2284

txts from the end of time

Niall McGrath

abuddhapress@yahoo.com

ISBN: 9798879850840

Niall McGrath © 2024

®™©

Alien Buddha Press 2024

First published March 2024

Alien Buddha Press ©™®

The moral right of the author has been asserted. A catalogue record for this book is available from the British Library. All rights reserved. No part of this publication may be transmitted in any form or by any means, electronic or mechanical, including photography, recording or any information storage or retrieval system, without permission in writing from the publisher. The book is sold subject to the condition that it shall not, by way of trade or otherwise, be lent, sold or otherwise circulated without the publisher's prior consent in any form or binding or cover other than that in which it is published and without a similar condition, including this condition, being imposed on the subsequent publisher.

The author has asserted his right to be identified as the author of this Work in accordance with section 77 and 78 of the Copyright, Designs and Patents Act 1988.

Any person who commits an unauthorised act in relation to this publication may be liable to criminal prosecution and civil claim for damages.

To:

Alice, Leigh, Juliet, Peter, Darryl, Rob, Cameron, Daniel and all the Oz Ts

The following is a work of fiction. Any similarities to actual people, places, or events, unless deliberately expressed otherwise by the author are purely coincidental.

one - txts from the edge

Tomás – what's up babe? where are you?

Ailbhe – on a precipice

Tomás - ?

Ailbhe – literally

Ailbhe – Cruachbán

Tomás - ?

Ailbhe – one of the peaks in MacGillycuddy's Reeks

Tomás – yikes - I'll not interrupt you if you're swinging off a mountainside

Ailbhe – taking a break – perched on a ledge – but roped on yeah – did go for a swing about twenty minutes ago – usual routine – no sweat

Tomás – it's icy up there?

Ailbhe – one of highest peaks in Ireland so of course – that's why it's called Crauchbán too, cos it's snow-covered n white earliest and longest of the hills in this range – faces north, gets the cutting Arctic winds

Tomás – baltic?

Ailbhe – minus ten – maybe double with wind chill

Tomás – what the hell going up there when it's like that?

Ailbhe – that's the point lol – sun was shining earlier, delightful – and we're only getting a few days of snow these days thanks to climate change so may as well make the most of it

Tomás – have you been to the top?

Ailbhe – not far now – I've been up before, just not in snow

Tomás – who's with you?

Ailbhe – just me

Tomás – seriously babe – are you mad or what?

Ailbhe – just a day out in the hills lol

Tomás – maybe I should go – not distract you

Ailbhe – I'll start again in a mo before the limbs seize up

Tomás – just googled Crauchbán – it's the one with the bad reputation

Ailbhe – like meself lol

Ailbhe – have there been accidents here? I haven't heard and they tell you these things – usually

Tomás – not that that I can see – don't you know about the disappearances though?

Ailbhe – nope

Tomás – Ireland's Mount Shasta

Ailbhe - ?

Tomás – the place in California where people go missing

Ailbhe – tumbles?

Tomás – naw – people just disappear – with mates and they look round and the person has gone – on a plain slope of snow even, no wind, no storms, no rocky edges – within minutes of last being seen – no trace ever found not even boots etc as would be the case when eaten by animals or birds

Ailbhe - yuck

Tomás – sorry and you up the side of a mountain

Ailbhe – it happens

Tomás – not to you I hope

Ailbhe – aw – sweet

Tomás – come back down safe

Ailbhe – I will

Tomás – and come see me when you are

Ailbhe – would love to

Tomás – or will I come to Killarney?

Ailbhe – not tonight – by the time I'm down it'll be late and mammy wants me to go visit auntie Síle it's her birthday

Tomás – nice

Ailbhe – not really Síle's on a morphine driver so in and out of consciousness and terminal - sigh

Tomás – sorry to hear that

Ailbhe – happens

Tomás – tomorrow then?

Ailbhe – aye

Tomás – lie in? eleven? dander then lunch?

Ailbhe – sounds good

Tomás – stay safe babe

Ailbhe – yup see you tomorrow to hang out with

Tomás – as opposed to hang off the side of a mountain with

Ailbhe – lol!

Ailbhe – would you?

Tomás – ?

Ailbhe – hang off a mountain with me?

Tomás – never done much climbing – but willing to try

Ailbhe – hate heights?

Tomás – not particularly – did a couple of drops and enjoyed the exhilaration of that - didn't have to sort of did it for the craic

Ailbhe – you might do

Tomás – might hate heights? no

Ailbhe – no – you might do for me to hang out with more – places like mountain peaks – if you hang around me you may well be hanging out in such places

Tomás – as a climbing partner?

Ailbhe – practice on a wall first maybe to get the basics

Tomás – I'm an absolute beginner

Ailbhe – the fun stage

Tomás – and your stage?

Ailbhe – seasoned veteran I guess – I thought you army guys would do that sort of thing

Tomás – some do – special forces – I've only abseiled a few times - you know what you're doing that's good

Ailbhe – do I? lol

Tomás – see you tomorrow babe

Ailbhe – yup – mwah!

two – invisible kisses

It was 30th December 2022 when I unexpectedly got those texts from Ailbhe Gallogly, from her rockclimbing trip to MacGillycuddy's Reeks. It was a chilly Friday and I was on duty at the Curragh, being an army sergeant. As it was the Christmas period, it was quiet. I was in the office, organising the lads' base security patrols, but the tv was on in the background, *Die Hard* was playing. Lieutenant Katie Walsh was in her office, working away at her emails, even though I'd taken her in a coffee and said to come take a break. All I got was her usual enigmatic if pretty smile and a non-committal nod.

There was a subdued mood, like an ominous dark cloud hanging over the place, as if a shroud of negative energy was dousing us like an invisible fire blanket, for earlier in the month a young soldier had died in southern Lebanon while part of a peacekeeping convoy. His mate was flown home, injured. The first fatality we'd had for twenty years, so a grim time.

Ailbhe Gallogly, a UCD post-grad chemistry student from Killarney. Nearly twenty-three, so a few years younger than me. I'd met her in the Palace Bar, in the city centre, about a fortnight before. Her last gathering with research colleagues before splitting for the holidays, she'd said. They were sensible sorts, leaving early.

The lads I was with were the complete opposite: Packie O'Neill and Aodh Devlin already had their kecks on outside their trousers. Thankfully those boxers were Christmas ones, with Santa Claus and a

Christmas tree, brand new and box clean. They were in the process of getting a diplomatic reminder from me to tone it down. How they could still stand amazed me. I didn't want to know, didn't want to be responsible.

I suggested to them, 'Hey, Aodh, get a taxi to Packie's after this pint, or that cute girl of his will be sending out for a substitute.'

'Yooooo!' Aodh wailed and Packie joined in.

I was beside Ailbhe, moved away from the lads to be closer to her. She seemed the quiet sort, was slightly aloof from her friends. They looked a bit more the corduroy type than she did. She was in ankle-length, blue denim-look leggings, a checked shirt over a tee shirt, a Christmas sweater over one arm, pint glass in one hand.

'Soldiers?' she asked.

'How can you tell?'

'My cousin's a medic. James Bogue?'

I shook my head.

'Can't know everyone. James and I and our families were on a big holiday together, Gormanstown beach, when we were wee, about thirteen. The rest were on the sand, he and I raced up the dunes. Suddenly, we heard a crack. A rifle shot. We peered down into this bowl in the dune and there were two lads prone on their stomachs, shooting at coins in the sand wall. The soldiers called us over. James was dead keen to see their weapons. They showed us they were empty, let us look up the barrels, told him how to clean them, dismantle and reassemble.'

'He got the bug then?'

She nodded, then over the noise in the pub told me, 'For a while he was mad about guns and war movies. Then, all of a sudden he dropped the idea, said he wouldn't want to harm others. But just before he was to do his leaving cert, that film was out, *Hacksaw Ridge*.'

'The lightbulb flashed on?'

Ailbhe nodded. A colleague came over and told her he was heading home, another was waving from the door. I could see Packie and Aodh chatting merrily with some other people there. It was extremely noisy, so I suggested we slip away.

'What about a literary pub crawl?' Ailbhe smiled. She had the most attractive light brown eyes, they drew you in, mesmerically.

'How do you mean?'

'Well, you know this place was frequented by people like Kavanagh? We could head to Davy Byrne's. I don't mean go round all the literary pubs tonight, though! I have stuff to check for experiments in the morning, readings to take. But Byrne's is on the way to my digs.'

'Can do. I've never been there actually.'

'What?!'

'Bit touristy. Always bunged.'

'Not always. Almost my local. If I had a local.'

'Don't really need one for orange squash,' I teased her.

'Where are you living anyway?'

'I'm in digs with a crowd of other postgrads in Warrington Place, twenty minutes from there.'

'Don't know it. Cool, but don't know it.'

'You?'

'Oh, my place is way out in Newbridge. Near the base, you see. But I used to be in digs here so I know my way around Dublin.'

So we walked the five or ten minutes through the busy night-time Dublin city centre streets to the next pub. Leaving the Palace, Ailbhe put on her Christmas sweater. It was one of those pastel pink and light blue gingerbread ones.

As we walked, I asked her, 'What is it you do?'

'Postgrad research, chemistry, into methods of countering pollution.'

'That's so good. That you care about the planet, I mean.'

'Somebody needs to.'

'Everybody should do, not enough do. My kid brother Daniel is good at and keen on sciences and thinking about maybe an engineering angle, is already thinking of getting a career with an eco-energy firm. All these big companies are installing green energy systems. They will need serviced and maintained. It's the future.'

'True.'

We went in through the door at Byrne's pub. It was shoulder-to-shoulder. She shook her head and we shuffled back out onto the street.

'You're right,' she said. 'Bunged.'

'Some other time,' I said.

'Coffee at mine, instead, Tomás?' she suggested.

I nodded and we wandered the twenty minutes or so south-eastwards. We chatted about many things. The poor lad who was in the news, that I'd been to Lebanon in the past, comedians we liked, that she would be heading home to Killarney before long for Christmas with the family. That I would be on duty then and my wee Aoife would be at her mother's and while I would see her plenty of weekends, I wasn't bothered about the festive period. I'd take her to visit my folks on a day off, she'd get her presents then. Ailbhe cooed over Aoife's picture, even. Naturally, she asked what about the child's mother. Got the lowdown on the dreaded Chloe. The usual story. That I would be more careful in future, who I hung out with, hooked up with.

I expected her flatmates to be there, but the kitchen-diner was quiet. Ailbhe chatted away as she began making coffee and dug out some mince pies, put them on a plate. I had one.

'Your flatmates in bed?'

'All away.' Over her shoulder as she poured into mugs, she said, 'You can stay with me. Just to sleep.'

'Oh, I'll get a taxi.'

'You never will, this night.'

I thought about it. 'Too true. Okay.'

That was all there was about it. We sat down, drank coffee, chatted. I learnt we shared, you know, a mindset, values, whatever you want to call it. We chatted and chatted as if we'd know each other forever.

Until Ailbhe yawned. 'Bedtime!'

So we rinsed out the mugs, cleaned teeth at the bathroom sink. I used a finger, then washed well. While I was using the loo she disappeared into the bedroom. As she went, she paused, looked back from the door, 'In here.'

So after I was ready, I went into her bedroom. She was already sitting up in the double bed, just a bedside lamp on. She was wearing a white tee-shirt that had on it in red lettering, *call me when you get to hell so I know you made it okay.*

Ailbhe saw I was staring at the tee-shirt and laughed. 'I got this for the louts that just want to stare at your tits.' I laughed with her. She patted the duvet. 'Just to sleep.' She yawned again.

'Aye,' I assured her.

I stripped to my kecks and slipped in under the duvet. We looked into each other's eyes. 'Will you be warm enough?'

'It's roasting.'

Leaning over the side of the bed, she agreed, 'Yup, I'll switch off the lecky blanket.' I heard two switches and the lamp went off, too. 'Night.'

'Night,' I replied and lay back on the cold, soft pillow.

I conked out immediately. When I woke, the bedroom door was open, I could hear the shower through the bathroom door. I wondered should I try and go in, if that was what she wanted. I decided against it and lay where I was until she came out in a cloud of steam, brushing her long auburn hair.

'Morning Red!' Ailbhe shrilled.

'Hiya!'

'Want a shower, while I organise breakfast?'

'Or is there someplace nearby we can go?'

'If you're treating me?'

'Not something I usually do either,' I told her, 'but why not?'

'I'll still need more than one cup of coffee to get going,' she told me as I headed to the bathroom.

So when I came out and joined Ailbhe at the kitchen table, there was coffee ready. Strong, rich, tasty. I swigged it down for the awakening kick. Then we went to a nearby café for breakfast.

She chose the veggie option, so so did I.

'You don't have to just to please me,' she said.

'I like the lightness of this type of food,' I told her. 'Besides, I want to please you.'

She gave me a saucy smile. 'You please me, alright, soldierboy.'

After breakfast, we shared a taxi, dropped her off at her lab, before I headed back to the camp. I was on time, but Lieutenant Walsh was already there.

'Is this the taxi ride of shame?' she smirked.

'Missed the bus, too icy for the bicycle, ma'am,' I told her.

'Yeah, right, sergeant.'

I had given Ailbhe my number while we were in the taxi, had arranged to see her for dinner that evening. So there began the heady few days of meeting up, sleeping together at her place. The first flush of a relationship, the fun of getting to know someone new. And it was all the better for the fact that she wasn't put off by my baggage and I wasn't put off by anything I learnt about her.

And then Christmas eve came. I got away from the camp early, got to spend a few hours with her at her place. We ate a takeaway, made love, before she had to get a bus to the station and another home to Killarney. I offered to drive her, but she didn't want to put me to the trouble and had the bus tickets already anyway.

So kissing her goodbye, the warmth of her lips and cheek, the feel of her body as we embraced before she got the bus from the stop near her digs, was the last time I saw Ailbhe in real life.

During the Christmas period, she videocalled with me on Christmas Day. We spoke of our presents, mostly. I'd given her a silver Celtic knotwork pendant, she was wearing it, showed it off to me.
'I'll keep it under my tee-shirt,' she said, winking. 'To ward off rogues.'
'Maybe I'm immune to its powers,' I codded her.
'That's okay,' she grinned, 'you're not a rogue.'
'Glad to hear it, babe!'
The rest of the time it was just voicecalls or texts. But we chittered away like twin souls.
Ailbhe only told me the day before of her plan to go to MacGillycuddy's Reeks. 'I think I'll go up the hills,' she sighed.
'Hill walking?'
'I do rockclimbing. I'm in the uni club. There's a minibus party of us probably going to the hills tomorrow. Or I'll take my car.'
'You have a car?'
'Well, I share it with my sister. She has it most of the time. But she's at work tomorrow.' I knew her older sister Medhbh was a newly qualified doctor.
Ailbhe knew I was working myself, until the Saturday. We told each other we were looking forward to seeing each other again then. I was so happy, happy for the first time in a long time. Not least because I was older and wiser now and I knew people better, knew how to judge women

better. I knew Ailbhe was special. Special to me, anyway. Very special. And I was already taking the risk, like I hadn't for ages, because I had been too wary to, for so long.

You know the rest. How Ailbhe went to the mountains by herself because the others all backed out at the last minute. How Ailbhe texted me from a rest point on a ledge near the pinnacle of Cruachbán. How I didn't hear from her that evening, as I'd expected to.

I went to the restaurant where we were supposed to meet up. I waited. Ailbhe didn't show. She'd told me where she lived so I drove round there, not knowing what to find. I found a family in panic, met her folks in awkward circumstances. I felt sick to the gut, believing they might suspect me, the new boyfriend they'd never met, of mischief.

But the guards checked out my story, that I'd been on duty at the camp when she'd been in the mountains, that she'd texted me, that Lieutenant Walsh gave me a glowing vote of confidence.

She gave me a couple of days off and I joined Ailbhe's medic cousin James with the search parties in the Reeks.

But days drifted into weeks. Drifted into months. Winter became spring. All the while it was like an itch you can't scratch, not knowing what had happened to her. Hoping she'd show up or, at least that her body would be found so I could move on in my head, in my heart.

I went back and saw her folks a couple of times. I phoned her cousin James a few times. Always the same story: nothing.

Ailbhe was gone. She wasn't coming back. Inside, I had accepted the logic of the situation. Even if, instead of grief there was just numbness. This unending, unassuageable numbness.

three - txts from the end of time

Ailbhe – you there?

Ailbhe – you there, Tomás?
Tomás – Ailbhe?
Ailbhe – yup – blimey – you got through to me
Tomás – sorry I was out a jog, didn't take my fone, missed you earlier – where are you? how's things?
Ailbhe – I suppose you've forgotten about me
Tomás – No! Just – it's been ages – what happened to you? are you alright Ailbhe?
Ailbhe – I know I can explain – I haven't been deliberately ghosting you – I owe you an explanation
Tomás – only if you feel you need to
Ailbhe – how long's it been?
Tomás – you know, three months
Ailbhe – same for you as for me
Tomás – why wouldn't it be? were you hurt? haven't you been well? did you lose your memory? - everyone's been worried about you – especially me
Ailbhe – aw, sweet – sorry Red – couldn't help it – none of that - let me explain
Ailbhe – no easy way

21

Tomás – did you lose your memory? fell on Crauchbán, wandered off somewhere? some wee Kerry farmer take you in, hold you in an outhouse all this time? sorry I'm not trying to be flippant – seriously worried about what happened to you – so relieved you're okay – are you okay?

Ailbhe – I'm okay

Tomás – mentally and physically?

Ailbhe – I'm not nuts! and I haven't broken a leg or anything

Tomás – sorry – didn't mean to sound mean

Ailbhe - you don't – I know you well enough to know you're not mean

Tomás – just, you disappeared without a word

Ailbhe – aye, sorry – you were right you know

Tomás – how's that?

Ailbhe - about Crauchbán

Tomás – dangerous to be up a rocky precipice in the ice and snow in December

Ailbhe – that it's like Mount Shasta

Tomás – eh?

Tomás – are you winding me up now?

Ailbhe – no!

Tomás – I just tried foning you, couldn't get a signal - can you fone me, Ailbhe?

Ailbhe – no signal here either

Tomás – seriously?

Ailbhe – it's because of where I am – or rather when

Ailbhe – I'll try again some time but it's understandable – I've tried and tried so many times – I couldn't get anyone else either – only you, only this way

Tomás – where are you?

Ailbhe - Killarney

Tomás – thank goodness! your folks will be pleased to have you back

Ailbhe – they're dead

Tomás – what?! when? I saw them not that long ago

Ailbhe – years ago – it's like this you see – I'm not in 2023 like you – that time I went up Crauchbán I passed through some kind of portal – I remember a bright flash of blinding light as I when along one rocky pass but thought nothing of it at the time, except that I shivered and lifted my shoulders as I strode through it because it was hot and it felt like I was passing through a fire - when I got back down, my car had gone

Tomás – stolen!?

Ailbhe – taken away, I'm sure – because I wasn't there in December 2022 anymore to go back to it – my sister got it all to herself, likely

Tomás – oh aye, I remember now, the guards took your car a week after you went missing

Ailbhe – I couldn't retrieve it because when I walked down the road, it wasn't there – I had to hike all the way until I got to Kate Kearney's pub

Tomás – a right trek

Ailbhe – over five miles yeah – it was still there – but just a refreshment stop for climbers and walkers – when I'd got to the summit of Crauchbán all you can see is the mountains and loughs and Kerry was covered in snow so I didn't realise anything was different – I sat and caught my breath awhile, looking across the county – the snow was general all over Ireland lol - admiring the roseate sun and apricot clouds before descending

Tomás – to find your car gone

Ailbhe – yup – though one thing I noticed on the way back which I hadn't on the way up was a stonking great building complex complete with perimeter fences – I saw it from up the mountain, thought it strange

Tomás – what did you do when you got down and discovered your car gone

Ailbhe – tried my mobile but couldn't get a signal – and all my info was scrubbed! – except your texts that morning – there was no one else around so I had no option other than to start walking! first, I thought someone at the big complex would help me – when I got to the front gate, there were cameras but no sentries – I waved, tried to get attention, nothing – I read the sign and it said it was MacGillycuddy Remand Prison

Tomás – is there such a place?

Ailbhe – not where you are - I've learnt since a bit about the criminal justice system now – it evolves – becomes both tougher and softer in that there is more time and care spent on the individual to try to rehabilitate those who can be but also to deal with those who are lost causes

Tomás – is anyone a lost cause?

Ailbhe – moot point – what I mean is, serious crimes like violent crimes, murders, sexual offences, the Illicits as they're called here, are consulted on their sentence

Tomás – you what? I think I'll take a Get Out of Jail Free card, thanks!

Ailbhe – what I mean is, life means life here and there isn't a mere six or twenty years for murder – but you are consulted if you want to opt for execution instead of life incarceration – not everyone gets the option and sometimes when they're old they get a jab towards the end

Tomás – like putting down a dog that's past it or that's got the taste of blood?

Ailbhe – most facing life tend to opt for a quick end

Tomás – saves state money and the illicit doesn't have to hang around

Ailbhe – well it's what happens here - Though I heard of a case where a killer wanted to be executed but he hadn't given up where all the victims' remains were, so they wouldn't let him have it

Tomás – here? but you're still in county Kerry right?

Ailbhe – I'm trying to explain Tomás yes - anyway I didn't get any joy from the prison that afternoon, so I walked on

Tomás – to Kate Kearney's

Ailbhe – aye and there was a woman and a girl that was clearly her daughter behind the counter - I asked did they mind if I sat in there, that was okay – they were wearing these unusual tunics, I was too tired to think much about it – I asked for coffee with milk, what had they to eat? a pastie, the woman said, so I got a veggie pastie – I didn't know till later there was only veggie or similar ones – but when I went to pay, the woman asked me for credits, for my credit card – so I took out my credit card and she looked at it, muttered 2027? these old antiques won't work – I asked what did she mean then realised the expiry date on my card was 05 27 - and she got out a card that was a disc and blank and scanned it and I said I didn't have one and the woman thought I'd lost it and said I could have this one, what was my name and address so I told her but it didn't work – no such address – don't worry, she told me, a glitch in system, I'll keep your details, recharge when the system is alright – and there was a tv screen on the wall, the news was on, only the console, the screen was different looking – and when I sat down to have my coffee, my head swirling after the wind in the hills, I began to notice the strangeness – the hairstyles, the clothes, above all the content of the news itself – it was about the five CSes meeting in the capital, Madrid – I was thinking, isn't the EU hq in Strasbourg or Brussels – and they showed and referred to two women, two men and this flamboyant character - they were the heads of America, Ozania, Africa, Europa and Asia – all about a political summit to discuss ongoing measures to tackle the pollution of the oceans, how the CS of Ozania is particularly active on that as it is island landmasses and just because they puts the environment agenda top every time – how there's just this one government of the world though with five committee or cabinet members, one for each continent with one as wcs – world chief of state – or *wicks* - which rotates around the five continents every two years - and a couple in the place were discussing the flamboyant one – the man said, oh they's America's first herm CS - and I blurted out herm? and the woman said herm, you know - and I asked hermaphrodite? - and she didn't know what I meant and the man laughed and said that's the archaic root of the word yes – CS? I asked and he said you know, chief of state – anyway, then I noticed the date on the news programme on the console and I checked with them, they confirmed it, it was 30th December 2283 – so now it's 2284, Tomás, I'm stuck in 2284

Tomás –the year 2284? the future?
Ailbhe – aye!
Tomás – is that possible? are you sure have you not just bumped you head or something Ailbhe?
Ailbhe – it's been three months Tomás you think by now I'd know if it was just some crazy dream or hallucination
Tomás – is there anyone else there Ailbhe, you could give the fone too, I could talk to or text?
Ailbhe – I'm not in a loony bin, honestly – I'm not hallucinating – I've been here three months now, honey – and I want to get home
Tomás – okay, okay, I believe you – I know you wouldn't wind me up in a silly way like that – you have been missing three months
Ailbhe – I've been here in the future all this time, Tomás
Tomás – and I guess because you've been there that long you've tried to get back already
Ailbhe – yup – lots of research into that – no luck – to cut a long story short, last weekend I even went back to Crauchbán and up the same route, hoping to get back through the portal - but nothing happened, it was still 2284

Tomás – we went looking for you, your cousin James, me, rescue services – and were way up there and nada

Ailbhe – aw, sweet of you to try – to help my family – to care

Tomás – course I care – course we tried

Ailbhe – at least you didn't find my body

Tomás – I wish I could find your body now 😜

Ailbhe – steady on soldierboy! - ps no emojis here anymore

Tomás – righto – five big countries only – Europa's capital's Madrid? where else is capital?

Ailbhe – in America it's Panama City, in Oz it's Canberra, in Africa it's Bangui, in Asia it's Kathmandu

Tomás – and they can speak English?

Ailbhe – well it's known as German now but it's the main language yeah – there's a bit of Mandarin, some Russian, some Spanish, some French and heritage languages are retained as part of human culture but mostly its only academics bother with the dead languages other than German – I mean English

Tomás – why's it called German?

Ailbhe – because Germany adopted it due to its prevalence in use at the end of the 21st century as did other Europa regions like the Netherlands, Poland and so on and it spread and then just took over

Tomás – don't the English complain?

Ailbhe – Bretagna and Irlanda are both just an agricultural outpost of Europa now really they haven't much of a population – people live in villages or country areas now – there are few towns – there's no more than about two million in each island

Tomás - so how do you live? in the future – where do you stay – what do you do for money?

Ailbhe – first, like I said, they saw my name and address didn't work – so I sat and sat and it was near closing time and the woman said haven't you a home to go to and I burst out crying – I was so tired, from climbing and walking and I thought I was going nuts - and then I wondered maybe I'd fallen and banged my head and not remembered – so I asked the women could I go to a hospital or to the police – she didn't understand the word hospital, so I said I was unwell, a clinic? she got it then – or the police, guards, crimefighters I suggested – responders, she told me – so I went to the clinic and it was just like one in our time really and the practitioner – about your age – and he - Jon Hegarty – examined my head, no bumps, and before long I was gurning like a baby, telling him everything – luckily he half-believed me, either thought I needed my mind examined or I was genuine – see his aunt was researching into parapsychology, they're more advanced now than in our day – and he's an interest in it himself – so he got me a room in this house – there's these communal homes like nurse's homes or student rooms in our time – no one's allowed to be homeless or live on the streets they get rounded up

Tomás – luckily you got somewhere safe

Ailbhe – well there's next to no crime or violence now – you can't get away with it, see – it's not tolerated as you may have guessed from what I said earlier about the prison system

Tomás – harsh legal system?

Ailbhe – seems like a sensible one

Tomás – not like *Clockwork Orange*?

Ailbhe – nothing so sinister! though basically people haven't changed – but their better side has come to the fore a lot more – after the bad times

Tomás – when were they?

Ailbhe – last century – the twenty-second century – but that's another story

Tomás – is it very different?

Ailbhe – not really – people still live in nuclear families, unless they are young and working like us - and they're much more community orientated, plus there's less people no megalopolises anymore or overcrowded urban areas – things are more spread out

Tomás – the death of the suburbs?

Ailbhe – yup! they've long gone – there are village-like hubs

Tomás – and you've got a job already?

Ailbhe – no one hasn't got a role, a job, here – it's not called work, it's called service – everyone does service – to the community, to each other, to oneself

Tomás – I'm cool with that

Ailbhe – lol!

Tomás – what's your service? and is there sexual service?

Ailbhe – soldierboy! if you mean is there prostitution, no –well apparently there is a little for barter on the black market but even then there's very little of that – everyone's so obedient – staid as the Swiss - but generally there's a lot less nonsense as there are decent personal relationships - though generally it's much like the twenty-first century

– just there's a lot less need of it and what there is is more friends helping each other out

Tomás – sorry I didn't mean to stray into the unsavory – what are you doing?

Ailbhe – my education in chemistry to postgrad level means Jon helped me do a test and get the qualification so I can be employed as a scientist since that is my field and get other documentation so I'm legal and I got a role in environmental monitoring – which means I get to go out and about and see the countryside and walk and Tomás, Tomás, Irlanda is just as beautiful as it ever was more so even as I know its not polluted mostly and the world is recovering from the harm we did to it in our time

Tomás – but Ireland's not a country?

Ailbhe – the nation state has gone – Irlanda exists but like a county a region of a continent now Europa is the political unit or rather really the world is as it is also just a part of one world government - but politics is just public administration now there isn't the kind of nationalistic mindset of our time – once there's one world government there's no need for war and economic strife between regions – there's cooperative politics now – but also liberal pluralist democracy and freedom of speech and an evolution of the best of the American and Irish republican and European tradition of our time – the age of empires and imperialism has long gone – greed and self-aggrandisement either on the individual or community level aren't tolerated – very few now are on the make all the time like they were in our time, we've evolved as a species

Tomás – that's a relief

Ailbhe – in many ways life is so much better herenow - hey let me say in case I lose connection – I've managed to wire up with some lengths of metal wire to one of the contemporary charging bases – if I ever lose connection, I'm here and I'll try to get through to you again and I will keep trying to get back to my own time and I will always always love you

Ailbhe - er did I say that, Tomás – I know we didn't know each other very long but I did tell you about my horrible experience with Seamus and how I have been wary since but you came along and you are so together and aw sweet Jesus, Tomás

Tomás – it's cool Ailbhe I understand – yes I love you too

Ailbhe – o Tomás

Tomás – I feel like I've always known you, Ailbhe – after all I've been through too – I've told you about how that bitch Chloe – *blooming* Chloe – ugh!

Ailbhe – you've said enough already – don't be so hard on your babymama

Tomás – don't call her that! – don't mention her at all – I know sometimes I'm guarded

Ailbhe – all the time soldierboy

Tomás – well hell Ailbhe whatever but you don't know her

Ailbhe – what are you about to tell me, she's the past?

Tomás – aye, of course she is the bloody past

Ailbhe - like my past

Tomás – don't tell me about your past

Ailbhe – you know some of it already

Tomás – too much – more than enough

Ailbhe – forget about all that – all that matters is now

Tomás – which now?

Tomás – Ailbhe?

Ailbhe – I'm still here – I'm just stunned honey – wow big talk

Tomás – sorry

Ailbhe – don't be sorry - it's understandable

Tomás – you're so sweet – but seriously she's bad news

Ailbhe – you trust her with your daughter

Tomás – just – blood's thicker than water – maybe she won't

Ailbhe – won't?

Tomás – harm Aoife

Ailbhe – a mother wouldn't do that

Tomás – plenty have

Ailbhe – Tomás!

Tomás – ignore my scepticism about human nature, being a soldier – we're wasting time – time you may not have – tell me what 2284 is like

Ailbhe – sure

Tomás – like when you left Kate Kearney's what did you see?

Ailbhe – like I say I went to the clinic – I borrowed a car – they are just there and you pay credits to use one

Tomás – like dublinbikes the freewheeling system?

Ailbhe – exactly – so the cafékeep had a robotaxi sitting out back and got me credit for it as an emergency trip to the clinic and entered the destination details – automated driving of course the vehicle took me

33

there – she foned ahead so practitioner Jon was expecting me - I was able to sit back and see the view – they're antigravity or hover vehicles so there's no wear and tear on road surfaces – which are there for horse carriages or dextavehicles – like bicycles – or

Tomás – flying cars?!

Ailbhe – not quite *Back to the Future* hoverboards – though we have those too for kids but they're easy to fall off so not so popular even when used with footstraps – anyway the fields on the way to Killarney were different – not enclosed fields anymore – some are but a lot of land now if not forested is huge long strips for arable crop rotation but there are external hedges with windbreak strips of hedging staggered out from the left then from the right – automated machinery travels along the short left hand side of a strip, then the longer right hand side, then the longer left hand side, all the way to the short right hand strip at the far end – bloody miles like in Australia or someplace – but nice with high hedges and copses – a magical snowy beauty to me that evening as the sun was setting – there were buildings and I said to myself out loud what's that place? and the vehicle answered like Alexa told me it was a seed house, machinery unit and farm management office – I've visited one since – scientists agronomists work in them so fascinating farmers now are agronomists mostly though hands-on but they are environmental scientists it's so cool I must tell you more about that later but Tomás when I got to the clinic I got health assessed and Jon had even arranged for a room in a hostel for me – no hotels anymore they're all called hostels

Tomás – is that where you live now?

Ailbhe – I'm in Killarney – it's still called Killarney – I was given a cottage on the outskirts of town, about two hundred years old – small but functionable – built from local stone, roofed with heather, just like in the old old days – our time

Tomás – wow - given?

Ailbhe – allocated – it's a different type of economy

Tomás – socialist?

Ailbhe – cooperative – capitalism still predominates – even communist countries are really capitalist, just the state is the capitalist instead of the individual – no, it works best with competition – just, let's say a balanced economy, more akin to those of say Scandinavia in our time than China or the USA

Tomás – the whole world?

Ailbhe – the one world – but it's all connected – public administration the economy social structures personality types

Tomás – personality types?

Ailbhe – oh aye – that's recognised as very important – the world in our time was dominated by alpha males – who defined things in animal terms – they're alpha males everyone else is a beta male and there to serve them - or female and there to serve them except alpha females who are there to share some limelight with but not be completely dominated by – whereas political administration, business and other leadership is better served by having other personality types in charge especially sigmas, deltas and betas males and females or also omega and gamma women

Tomás – avoiding alphas?

Ailbhe – wherever possible – it depends on the individual of course – and people now are taught to be more self-reflective so usually alphas are less egoistic easier to work with

Tomás – I wonder which am I? us soldierboys usually think of ourselves as alphas, right?

Ailbhe – hm Tomás I think you're definitely a sigma

Tomás – better than being a tiresome alpha like someone like Trump - and you?

Ailbhe – what do you think?

Tomás – definitely an alpha female!

Ailbe – the jury's out on that one

Tomás – didn't they psychoanalyse you when you got there?

Aiblhe – yeah but I never asked what I was – yet - and another thing - no matter what Tomás – no matter what – I love you – even if I don't get back – no matter what happens

Tomás – no matter what, Ailbhe, I love you

Ailbhe – but I'm going to research more and work with people to see if I can come up with a way of getting back to our time

Tomás – I get you – don't fret, Ailbhe – just do what you can

Ailbhe – I miss my mom and dad and sister and even James and all of yous

Tomás – I get you – I miss you, sweetie – so much

Ailbhe – sometimes I wonder why am I here – was it just by chance, walking into a portal by accident – or was it meant to be

Tomás – don't say that love

Ailbhe – if meant to be, was it a test, of me, or us, so that I am a better person or we are better people for the experience, when I get back or – was it meant to be I'm here for ever

Tomás – remember that old Sitcom, you might have seen it on some satellite tv channel somewhere, *Goodnight Sweetheart*

Ailbhe – I've seen a couple of episodes, Gary goes back from the 1990s to the 1940s, wartime Britain

Tomás – yup, through a portal - which tells me, if you can go one way, you can go another

Ailbhe – maybe real life isn't like tv sitcoms

Tomás – all the same, it should be possible, it's only logical

Ailbhe – true – but I've already tried going back to the portal I came through, I've been back to the mountain

Tomás – maybe it's you, you are susceptible, so if you go to where and when a portal is strong, you get through – try again, Ailbhe?

Ailbhe – I will

Tomás – it's just a matter of timing – you'll get back, Ailbhe

Ailbhe – thanks for that, Tomás, I'll try again – I can envisage a bright, warm spring or summer day, glistening heather, beautiful scenery, the whole vista below me from the mountains – I'll try climbing there again

Tomás – that's the stuff

Ailbhe – I don't want to go now in case I never get in contact with you again, Tomás

Tomás – same here

Ailbhe – but I have work

Tomás – I understand – me, too

Ailbhe – I'll recharge up my fone battery

Tomás – yup okay

Ailbhe – if I can

Tomás – please god

Ailbhe – no matter what

Ailbhe – I'll txt again when I can

Tomás – I'll try to be receptive

Ailbhe – that's all a man can do – try

Tomás – 😜

Ailbhe – lol!

Tomás – just know, I'm here for you

Tomás – because I care about you

Ailbhe – hell, Tomás – this is so unfair on you – you didn't sign up for a long distance relationship – you're a man in his prime I can't be doing this to you

Tomás – don't worry about me – it's you we need to get back here where you belong

Ailbhe – I'll be working on that

Ailbhe - see you – bye – maybe this how it ends not with a bang but a whimper

Tomás – I'll be here for you Ailbhe - no matter what

Tomás – Ailbhe?

four – without trace

I was in the office just after Ailbhe's texts stopped, when Lieutenant Walsh came in asking for paperwork. I responded perfunctorily. There was only us two, it being lunchtime. After her business was done, she approached closer, to the edge of my desk.

'You seem to be on a downer, Tomás. Trouble with the ex?'

'Why ask that?'

'That's what it usually is, with my guys.'

I shook my head. 'I've a friend seems to be in trouble. Not the,' I gestured with my hand a bump in front of my stomach, 'kind.'

'Drugs?'

I shook my head again. 'More her mind.'

'The one that's been missing? Ailbhe?'

'You even remember her name, ma'am?'

'Sure. Is she back?'

'Sort of is and isn't. Didn't you know a guy in the police corps, ma'am?' She perched on the edge of my desk, in her tight pencil skirt and white blouse. I could feel the heat off her, smell her perfume. 'I have contacts everywhere. Hm, there's Egan there, yes.'

'The guy with the contacts in the forensic science lab?'

'Lieutenant McCarthy, yeah. You think he can help?'

'I was wondering if he could. See, I've had texts.'

'From Ailbhe? She's alive? Where is she?'

'This is the thing.'

'She won't say?'

'Can't or won't. I think she might have banged her head. I didn't know her very long. Yet I feel responsible, somehow.' Katie was nodding. 'If the forensics guys could track her mobile, we could find her.'

Katie slithered around, moved my screen and keyboard, dialled into the connectivity system, put it on speaker. 'Hi, Egan, Katie Walsh here and I'm on speaker.'

'Lieutenant Walsh! A pleasure. How's things at the Curragh?'

'Quiet, thank goodness. I need a favour? I have Sergeant Roe with me, you know Tomás whose friend went missing while rock climbing, it was in the media?'

'Yeah, of course.'

'You've mates in the forensics lab, haven't you? Could they track her mobile from connection with his?'

'We're not the FBI, but I can do things most people wouldn't believe.'

'Oh, Egan, I can believe some of the things you can do are unbelievable.'

They shared a saucy giggle. 'When can he come round?'

'No time like the present.'

'Cool. Thanks mate. I have a meeting with the commandant shortly, but I'll send him over now. Cheers, m'dear.'

I clicked my mouse to end the call. 'You don't mind me going there now?'

'It's quiet, Tomás, you can catch up on things when you're back laters, tomorrows.'

'Thanks you so much. As I said, I hardly knew the girl, but just, not finding her body, then this. I guess I should tell the guards, too.'

'Sure check it out first, see if you can find her. If they get something, let that detective lad…'

'Marty Murphy.'

'Yeah, let him know if you get anything worthwhile.'

'Her texts were pretty out there, sounded like she was disturbed. Or more likely someone else had found the thing and was playing silly buggers. But I feel it should be checked out.'

'Sure, sure,' Lieutenant Walsh cooed, leaning forward to stroke my arm gently. She was flicking her pendant back and forth again in a casual, seductive way. 'And if there's anything, anything at all I can do for you, if you need any help at all, you know where to find me.'

I smiled up at her, nodding. Wondering.

'Sign out a land rover. See what they can discover.' She slid off the desk, skirt riding up some before she smoothed it down again as she strode briskly from my office space. 'And let me know how you get on. Intriguing, Tomás.'

'It's certainly that.'

'What we signed up for, eh, a bit of adventure, a bit of excitement?'

With that she was gone and so was I, down the road to the labs. At the reception at Garda headquarters in Phoenix Park in the city, I asked for Egan McCarthy and he soon met me, got me a pass and signed in and led me to the communications lab. He knew his way around the place as they provided support to the military police corps.

'It's an open case, so any help will be great. So she's made contact?'

'The thing is, Lieutenant McCarthy, it's complicated.'

'Nothing's really complicated, in my experience. You just break it down into its constituent parts. If we think a situation is complicated, usually it's because someone doesn't want to accept the facts, things as they are, is trying to duck issues. Or what they consider to be an unpalatable scenario or solution. Often, it's just a matter of taking the emotions or prejudices out of the thing.'

'Can we get a search done of mental institutions and hospitals for anyone around the time she went missing or since being admitted with memory loss and the kind of hallucinations she's been exhibiting?'

The Lieutenant assured me, 'I have done three such sweeps since she went missing. We'll do another. This contact is the most promising lead so far. Technology rules,' he added, directing the comment at the woman we were joining.

The forensic scientist with us asked sarcastically, with a wink, 'What's he blethering on about?'

I was instantly mermerised. Was this some crazy or cruel joke they were all playing on me? She was the spit of Ailbhe. I blinked at first, thinking it was Ailbhe, had to stare at her to notice the slight difference in age, height and build. The most striking resemblance between them was her shocking blue crystal eyes.

'This is Aideen Rourke, the guru with mobiles.'

We shook hands.

Egan stuttered, 'Sorry Aideen, but there's an uncanny resemblance between you and the missing woman. What a weird point of synchronicity.'

'Yeah!' I laughed out of embarrassment or awkwardness, 'Bit of a double take there for me.'

Aideen waved a hand, 'I can assure you, I'm no relative nor have I heard of these people. Coincidences happen.'

'I'm sure you are a very different person.'

Smiling she told us, 'I had a boss once, she had an office to herself and the desk and walls around it were plastered with pictures of Leonardo di Caprio. I looked and looked for a picture of her family and there was one, her husband with the two kids. And he was the spit of Leonardo!'

Egan laughed, 'She had a type! Regardless of personality.'

Aideen gestured towards me, 'But you're anxious to know about this missing woman, Sergeant Roe.'

'The thing is,' I told them, 'either Ailbhe's had a knock on the head or someone has found her phone and is jerking our chains, or…'

'Something unpalatable?' Egan asked.

'Or incredible.'

Nodding, I handed them my mobile. Aideen inserted a cable and displayed my texts from Ailbhe on her desk screen. I waited for their reaction.

'I wouldn't want to abandon the poor woman, even if she is stuck in a timewarp,' I half-joked as they read the end of the series of texts.

Aideen smiled. 'Why don't you lads go get a coffee. Then when you get back I'll tell you where she is. Or where her mobile is, at any rate.'

So I went with Egan to the canteen area. We got coffee from a machine, Egan got himself a bag of Tayto potato crisps. We sat at a café style table, facing each other.

'Do I even want to find her, if she's nuts?'

'Sounds like you do, from the texts. Sorry, I don't mean to be unkind. It's very nice, actually, touching. We're all like that with those we are close to. Even if we try not to show it, sometimes. Especially in our line. The macho military.' I creased an eyebrow, to which he responded, 'I'm not soft. Just, we're not infantry. And our daily business exposes us to the depths of human sentiments. Much of it ugly, stupid, nasty. Some of it heart-breaking. I've just concluded a case of child abuse.' He shook his head, wincing.

'I get you, sir. Being on the front line, like we were in Lebanon, you experience things, like the poverty people endure, the meanness, as you say, of violence and of societies when they don't really value a person much, any individual person, or other living creature. Anyway, what do you think?'

'You've covered the most logical explanations. Aideen will crack this, wee buns to her.'

'So, you're friends with Lieutenant Walsh?'

He nodded. 'Katie and I came through basic training together.'

'She seems lively.'

'Seems? You work with her.'

'But when someone is your boss, and you're in an office, it's all professional talk, mostly. You don't learn much about then, really.'

'I don't think I could ever fathom Katie Walsh. Flirty but harmlessly so, not really at all the badass she pretends to be. She's a force of nature. As Ailbhe Gallogly seems to be. I mean, to go rockclimbing on your own, in the winter snow.'

'Not *that* unusual.'

'True. But. Anyway, if it is her mind, why project the future? I'm speculating. Did a psychology degree, see. With a masters in criminal psychology.'

'Impressive.'

'Whereas you,' he indicated my sniper's badge, 'have equally useful skills. At least for your field.'

'Thanks. I'm beginning to wish I'd done what James did, Ailbhe's cousin, and trained as a medic.'

'Oh, that's much too dangerous!' Lieutenant McCarthy drained his disposable cup and rose to his feet. I followed him back to the lab.

When we reached Aideen's desk, she looked ready to report. 'It's like this. Where is, or when the texts were made where was, Ailbhe's mobile? No idea.'

Egan McCarthy sighed. 'Untraceable?'

'Should be traceable,' Aideen said. 'Should be possible to say where, when. There is trace for her going from Killarney by car, judging by the speed, to MacGillycuddy's Reeks, on the 30th December. Then, a slow meandering in the hills, as she climbs. Then, it goes blank. All trace lost. There should be metadata for when the texts were sent after that, but there's nothing.'

'How unusual is that?' Egan asked.

'Usually you can tell if signal is lost, or malfunction has occurred. This kind of scenario, where the mobile is operating enough to allow texts to be sent and received but there's no notation for where and when, unprecedented, as far as I know. I just don't understand it.'

'So we can't prove even that it is 2284, as she says?'

Aideen smiled. 'She's in no time, no place, so far as the data shows.'

'She is in a timewarp, after all,' I whispered, almost believing it.

Aideen handed me back my mobile. 'If you get anything more, call me directly and come back here yourself. I'd love to have another go. You never know, there might be a little bit more to go on. And I don't like to be beaten.' She winked.

Egan escorted me to the reception desk. As I was signing out and handing back my visitor's pass, he said, 'What a nuisance. Not being able to find anything to go on. I thought we had her, there. I thought it was going to be simple, would tell us she was in Killarney at a friend's house or something. Sorry we couldn't crack it.'

'No signal, or not strong enough might mean in the mountains some place, like say some wee drunk's or hermit's den.'

'Not the kind to usually play games like codding someone they're in the future. And you only try it with one person, not some of her other friends, too.'

'Perplexing, yes. I suppose you think I'm nuts, now, too, for even considering it might be true?'

'It's not logical. Because we've never proved it can be done. But there are tales of weird things, there are always stories of things that are on the edge. Like, my mate Marty Murphy in the guards, his team used a psychic once. To trace a missing child. She was able to say which area of woods to search in, and some details, when they found the remains, were spot on. How do you explain that? Luck? Chance? Coincidence? My oul' grannie used to say, nothing happens by chance. I didn't listen to it then. After seeing some of the things I have, I'm beginning to wonder.'

'I'm beginning to wonder, should I go up there. Crauchbán. See if I can either find her remains, or…'

'There was an extensive search. Could be like looking for a needle in a haystack. My experience tells me for things like that, just wait and some time she'll show up. Her body, if she's lost. Or, if she's hiding out, she will herself.'

'They never found that guy Irvine who went missing on Everest a hundred years ago.'

'They did find Mallory.'

'But not for three quarters of a century. I won't be here if it takes that long to find Ailbhe.'

'Point taken. I've done some rockclimbing. If you want, I'll go with you Saturday?'

'Really?'

'Sure. Actually, I must confess, I'm more interested in seeing if there is some kind of portal. Or does that make me sound mad?'

'No. I was thinking the same thing myself.'

'But you have a kid, don't you, Sergeant? Katie told me. If I zap into the future never to return, it doesn't really matter, there's no one left to miss me here. But you have family.'

The guy behind the reception desk was giving us peculiar looks. So I just grinned, shook hands, told Egan I'd see him Friday evening, made my way back out to the land rover.

The cold air hit me and I decided to nip back in to use the loo before driving back. When I was passing through the foyer, I saw Egan still chatting to the receptionist, with his back to me. Neither of them saw me as I was passing by to the corridor where the restrooms were. As I passed, I thought I overheard them gossiping.

The receptionist seemed to be saying, 'Do you think he's faking it? Even unconsciously?'

Egan's shoulders shrugged. 'Why would he? Grief?'

When I returned from the gents, Egan was gone back to his own office or back to see Aideen and the receptionist was busy checking his screen and still did not notice me. So I left unacknowledged.

Egan was as good as his word. He picked me up after dinner on Friday evening. It was a four hour drive down the M7, through Limerick. We shared a room in a B&B near the Reeks. Got up early, had a big fry up, to fuel up, before checking our equipment and driving towards Crauchbán.

As we were making our way up the first part, Egan asked, 'Yous think you found her route, when you were here last, searching?'

'When I check where we went with the data Aideen did get from Ailbhe's mobile, I know we went the right route. And from where the data ends to where the summit is, it's a clear route. She texted me from a ledge.' I pointed it out to him, way up on the jagged hillside. 'It's just after that the data ends. If there is a portal, we should be there in about five hours' time.'

So we climbed, steadily and carefully. It was a good day, not cold and icy as it was when Ailbhe had been there in December. We even rested at the ledge she had, had some warm sugary tea and a bite to eat, before trying to pinpoint the portal area.

It was while we were resting on the ledge Egan told me, 'I emailed a report to Marty Murphy, in the guards. About the texts and mobile data. Not the content of the texts, just that she or someone had been in touch. But that the place and exact time could not be established. He just replied with the usual line, a thanks for keeping us informed and let us know of any further developments.'

'Thanks for not telling him she claims to be in 2284!'

'I'd be more embarrassed than you.'

'It wouldn't embarrass me.'

'Well, no, that's not the right word. Anyway, there's no need, is there. At this stage. Unless we discover something. Something of scientific importance.'

'Even if we did, few would believe it.'

'I'd find it difficult to believe myself.'

'I prefer not to think about it, just try and find out the way of it all. What's happened to Ailbhe?'

We had to scale a steep short face with ropes. We checked our readings on Egan's gps smartwatch and as we clambered over an area of loose rocks, he pointed ahead.

'Between here and the next six metres, it should be here.'

'There's a valley isn't there, you can't really go any way but this route ahead. So she came here. There's nowhere to fall from here.'

Egan looked to the edge of the mountain. 'Unless she was disorientated and went over that way.'

'That area was thoroughly searched,' I told him. 'I remember it well. If she'd gone down there anywhere, we'd have found her. Now the snow's gone, you can see there's nothing there.'

'When it melted, it might have carried a body down further and it could have gone in more than one direction and, sorry to be so crude, but, you'll know, scavengers might have disposed of any remains. Or most.'

'Not boots and clothing and, and her mobile.'

'We'd see something,' he pointed out.

We stared at one another, taking a deep breath, knowing we were about to pass through the portal area. Egan went first. I followed.

Nothing happened.

We carried on, reached the summit. Egan got me to take a picture of him there, took a selfie with me there, took one of me up there to send to me. When we got back to the portal area, Egan paused, stood there, right in the heart of the area. He sent the pictures to me from his mobile. My phone, in my pocket, beeped for each picture received. Even away up there, in the wind-beaten rocks.

Looking down over the Kerry landscape, gazing out over the deep blue loughs and stark green of the lower northern countryside, I wondered if I'd ever hear from Ailbhe again. If I would ever find her.

I asked Egan, 'How many people go missing every year?'

'About four thousand. Less than point one percent of the population.'

'How many are never found?'

'About twenty a year. That's about half a percent, of those who go missing. In the USA, it could be between point one and point two of a percent of the population go missing.'

'But every one is someone. Most leave people behind, wondering.'

'People like you.'

As we began making our way gradually back towards the flatland, I quipped wryly, with a touch of gallows humour, 'Are we just statistics? Or are we human?'

five – txts from herenow

Tomás – hey, Ailbhe, how's things?
Tomás – are you there?

Tomás – how are you, Ailbhe?

Ailbhe – sorry I didn't respond your messages, it's been difficult to get charged up - for me to make a connection

Ailbhe – are you about, Tomás?
Tomás – hey, Ailbhe, I'm here – are you still there?
Ailbhe – yup I'm here – still on the other side
Tomás – it's so good to hear from you again – how's things? any joy with sorting your return?
Ailbhe – Jon Hegarty, the practitioner, has done so much research for me – we found these parapsychologists, they knew of spells from ancient traditions that were supposed to help – but that didn't help me - I've tried loads of different things Tomás but nothing's worked
Ailbhe – yet
Ailbhe – but I'm going to keep trying
Tomás – I went with a detective friend back to Crauchbán
Tomás – we climbed the route you went – found the place where the portal should be – passed through there – nothing – just like when we searched for you in December

Tomás – so how come you were transported but we weren't?

Ailbhe – I can't explain that, Tomás – don't you believe me?

Tomás – you expect any one to believe such a tale?

Tomás – the guards believe you are a third party who has Ailbhe's phone and is playing a silly game – you're wasting police time, you'll get taken to court – they have a trace on my mobile, they will find you

Ailbhe – I hope you do find me! I want to get back to you, Tomás – I wish you didn't think I was someone else or mad – this situation is driving me mad but because I'm stuck here – I know its unbelievable – but I have to believe it because I'm here – I have to keep my sanity to survive – I wouldn't trick or prank someone, not this long, not like this, that's way too nasty and mad

Tomás – I'm sorry Ailbhe – you know I believe you – it's just hard to do so when these investigators are doubting it

Ailbhe – one thing Jon did was or that he got the experts here to do was try and trace your mobile signal find out where you are – but there's no trace of you or your phone signal

Tomás – not even from the day we were in touch when you were up the mountain, 30 Dec?

Ailbhe – I only have records back to after I got here, in this century, on the afternoon of that day – everything prior to my getting here in this timezone has been wiped

Tomás – strange

Ailbhe – too right

Tomás – we tried the same but you know that already

Ailbhe – how would I know that?

Tomás – sorry

Ailbhe – trying to catch me out as if I am someone who knows about your investigation and is codding you?

Tomás – no no Ailbhe just you're in the future – is there no record of your going missing etc

Ailbhe – there are media articles about the case true – lost without trace, that's me – if you must know btw my death certificate is formalised in early 2030 after seven years missing

Tomás – oh Ailbhe – you looked that up?

Ailbhe – why not – it's not real, anyway – there's just a big gap between the old me and the new

Tomás – did you look me up – apart from my grave that you went to – what I made of my life

Ailbhe – not right away – but yes – but I'm not going to tell you anything about that – however hard you ask

Tomás – no worries babe que sera sera! - well it goes without saying I'm not still around in your new time, unless there's some fantastic progress in medical science that means we can survive for much longer

Ailbhe – life expectancy now is just like it is for you – up to about eighty for most, a few making it to one hundred

Tomás – have you at least settled in, made friends?

Ailbhe – I have a place in the apartments, if that's what you mean – most people live in detached cottages or bungalow complexes in villages almost like folds – you get a place to stay as part of your salary but you do own it the rent is affordable and is a kind of mortgage, so you have responsibility for the place, I hope to get one soon – they thought it would be better for me for a while to live with others to get to know people rather than be alone – the wee houses have gardens for growing vegetables and are like many in your time a kitchen-diner, living room, washroom, bedroom and spare room for guests or as a workspace or research room and storage - most of those around me here are decent folk – most are nowadays – and I see some from work socially too – I've tried the squash and tennis clubs and of course the climbing club – there's quizzes, snooker, dramas

Tomás – live theatre? films?

Ailbhe – there are communal big screens in most apartment blocks for the residents, others can come in depending what's on – or the news – there isn't twenty-four hour news but regular bulletins and special bulletins if something big has happened

Tomás – such as

Ailbhe – an earthquake – death of a famous person – they still have the Olympics so sporting news big wins

Ailbhe - they show old movies too at all times of the day or old tv programmes – you can do requests from a central library – I have done that a few times, introduced people to stuff I knew, that they would not have thought to try watching as it's so old – like the *Walking Dead, Downton Abbey, Pretty Little Liars* and *Hannah Montana* – cried my lamps out with nostalgia

Tomás – what did they make of Downton Abbey?!

Ailbhe – like what we'd make of something about Napoleonic times or Tudor times – how odd it was way back then

Tomás – figures

Ailbhe – hey I found some pop music vids - my mam used to play Bananarama's *Venus* when I was wee and it came on - she and me and my sister used to dance round the living room to it - so I was dancing round the place like a toddler - really astounded them all guess they saw me like we would some loose nineteen-twenties flapper girl ha!

Tomás – baby you've got!

Ailbhe – yeah baby I've got it – hey Tomás I went back up Crauchbán again myself you know several times tried to go when the atmosphere was right the same time of the lunar cycle all that no matter what circumstances we tested nada

Tomás – we?

Ailbhe – some friends – Jon or Carla or

Tomás – Jon the doctor?

Ailbhe – he's the local doctor so yes still see him – he counsels me for my emotional balance

Tomás – wish I had you here for my emotional balance

Ailbhe – aw Tomás – you know if you need comfort that's understandable I'm here you're there

Tomás – I wouldn't do that to you Ailbhe - have there been any other cases of people disappearing there?

Ailbhe – only the vague tales of strange happenings – obviously my case is one of those that's now cited

Tomás – how does the good doctor react to your claiming to be someone from the past?

Ailbhe – Jon? he likes to hear about life in our time – takes it in his stride – what I can tell him impresses him I think he might even almost believe me - there are a few other cases since but the only really documented one since mine wasn't until 2066

Tomás – another 43 years if I'm still around I'll be 80 crikey – will I still be around?

Ailbhe – naughty soldierboy – though I will tell you I visited your grave once – collapsed in a heap and wept my lamps out – my parents' too and my sister's and all her family – I saw their dates of death, I know how long they've got – if you dwelt on it too much it would crack you up – I won't tell you, Tomás, that wouldn't be fair – but you're buried with your wife and even your kids are there – not Aoife, your future family and some of their ones

Tomás – wow heavy! – say don't be upsetting yourself Ailbhe – maybe you get back here

Ailbhe – there's no future trace of me after I disappear – no record of my reappearing then – sorry to break this to you but you have a right to know – doesn't seem like there's any hope for me – I'm gone for good – so you have to get over me forget about me

Tomás – no! never!

Ailbhe – well you have to come to terms with the fact that we are apart for good – as I say, you do, I know, because you do marry again

Tomás – well I don't know about that even if that were to happen it might be out of you know loneliness or carnal necessity it wouldn't change how I feel about you Ailbhe - so long as you can keep in touch txt from the end of time I'll be here to txt with you babe – jees I can hardly see my phone screen I'm bawling like a baby what's wrong with me

Ailbhe – I'm crying too love but Tomás even though it might be kinder just to break off now I won't while I can still get through I'll try because I can't just switch off loving you

Tomás – nor I you

Ailbhe – which is why I say you needn't wait for me

Tomás – all the same while I'm still able to get through to you I won't abandon you I won't betray you I love you so fiercely until the end of time

Ailbhe – aw and here I am as if at the end of time and if I can't be there with you at least I can tell you how it is now

Tomás – yeah Ailbhe tell me more about times to come – you said its better in the future?

Ailbhe – after the hard times and the bad times it has improved

Tomás – a different way of living – more equal sharing of resources sound like?

Ailbhe – yup – like here/now if you want a go on a luxury yacht, you just pay the credits

Tomás – no private ownership?

Ailbhe – there is because it's necessary because it instils responsibility in a way collectivism doesn't but not in quite the same way – there isn't the same greed the same fixation on profit motivation though – but there is reward for effort - like a guy in our research organisation gets some extra credits more as he is so good at what he does and has made useful discoveries he gets more credits than the managers and he wanted to treat his comp – companion -

Tomás – the old comp indoors!

Ailbhe – behave soldierboy – aye anyway companion – comp

Tomás – compo and cleggie?

Ailbhe – ha-ha – he wanted to treat his partner to a wedding anniversary so they bought a fortnight's cruise on a superyacht – its available to charter – no one owns their own that would be silly when you can hire one

Tomás – did they have to share?

Ailbhe – no – full crew just for them – they could take friends too if they wanted and most take a big extended family group but they wanted it to be romantic and just the two of them so they went for it – but people share credits too – lend or give credits to others – if you are short of credits and haven't been completely mad with them you just get more like say if you were a hundred short for the cruise of a lifetime on a superyacht they'd just give you the discount probably or give it you on loan to pay off over the next while if you could – but the idea of having only billionaires owning the superyachts that's long gone

Tomás – does sound like a much nicer time – fairer

Ailbhe – oh yeah way better at least the world has something to look forward to even if there is still all the shit of the twenty-first and twenty-second centuries to go through first and the beginning of this one, the twenty-third – suffering caused by the human race, of course – you know Tomás there are still some old families living in ancestral homes, big houses, and they get help if they need it as its preserving heritage – though usually have open days too to let people see an historic place – like the way I can walk in the grounds of Muckross House still

Tomás – I'll check it out sometime soon - and it's the same for everyday things you said like food – by the way I'm just going to chat away until you have to go – and when I get you back on here I will do the same – just keep in touch with you while I can

Ailbhe – in case we can't any more – I know – until we can't if that comes – it may Tomás just to warn you as the communal phones here charge in a different way and my ad hoc wiring up to get power to this one is hit and miss and when this old thing goes that could be it forever – so I'll say my goodbyes now in case we get cut off suddenly sometime without warning

Tomás – sorry to be morbid but its like death isn't it – a sudden severing of communication – I get what you mean though – so know I say the same to you – much love and forever in my heart

Ailbhe – much love my love – aye – agriculture and food production – much improvement there – had to be for the sake of the environment – of course in our own time they were beginning to catch on to the harm we were doing to our world to the ecology – slowly but there you go

Tomás – should we all be eating less meat as they say?

Ailbhe – from the perspective here of the 23rd century farming is done in harmony with nature and with other sentient creatures – here its like India I guess – cattle are treated as sacred, you care for them and let the calves take milk first, then take only what's left – people usually drink oat milk so dairy products are more for children who need more calcium - people have sheep but only for wool – they roam the hillside and are shorn but left to breed – they are looked after, sometimes milked by country people or for cheese – but animals aren't killed for meat no – hides are kept after they die for leather – natural materials are used there's virtually no plastic anymore except for special uses like in medical equipment where glass, wood or other things just can't be used

Tomás – they've banned plastic? not a moment too soon

Ailbhe – much too late, the planet's still choked by that horrid stuff especially the seas

Ailbhe – there's much more forestation as so much more wood is needed – the right kind of trees too – for carbon sinks as well as for use in building or whatever it is – in your time only 11% of Irlanda was covered with trees

Tomás – isn't that good?

Ailbhe – more than for about 350 years, but a lot more was needed as carbon sink – before we started to use it for building and so on and before the English came in 1172 for it, it was about 80% and a squirrel could travel from Malin Head to Brow Head without leaving the branches - around 1600 it was only 20% tree coverage

Tomás – how much in your time?

Ailbhe – my time – I haven't got used to calling it that yet – I guess I should huh? – I'm not sure of the exact figure herenow but I think it's near the 30-35% mark – with a lot of space given to solar farms and turbines – as I was saying livestock is kept but for post-death byproducts – bonemeal for fertilizer, leather – the cows are kept their natural lifespan, twenty years, not forced to overproduce and expend themselves in a few years – because they produce the same over twenty years as over six the other way which is unnatural, wasteful and unnecessarily cruel – so cows are kept almost like pets – people care for and respect the animals they have herenow

Tomás – my uncle's a farmer, I used to stay with them for the summer – they care about their stock too

Ailbhe - I know but not quite in the same say – its not quite the same spiritual connection as in Hindu society but not far off it – you don't really care about them if you're willing to send them to an abattoir eh? its more of a vegetarian or lacto-vegetarian kind of agriculture

Tomás – and that works, economically?

Ailbhe – it does now – there was a transition period where it was difficult – around or just after the bad times – the hard times was the economic travails of the 21st century, the bad times was the warring and struggle for resources of the 22nd century – after the bad times, the new order was established

Tomás – you're trying to tell me there isn't greed anymore? or political corruption?

Ailbhe – the education system is much better – people do environmental sciences, food production, philosophy, psychology things like that at an earlier age so they understand themselves and how society works at an earlier age and better – so there are fewer ignorant, greedy, vain people – there was one group got into power a few decades back, nearly overthrew the new order just as it was working well after the bad times – but people saw the danger and a bit like the avoiding of the worst effects of 6th January 2021 in the USA from resulting in dictatorship sense prevails herenow – there's still capitalist competition in the economy, you can't escape that and indeed an element is healthy, makes the system work efficiently, but there needs to be balance and you get that herenow too

Tomás – and there's no war?

Ailbhe – the bad times was a long period of dreadful war and famine – it ended with the new order of the world government which has gradually organised things so that the new cooperative economic system works – they did manage to avoid the kind of f up that Lysenkoism achieved – you heard of him?

Tomás – no

Ailbhe – Soviet agronomist – his silly ideas led to famines in the USSR and China in the twentieth century that meant millions died of starvation

Tomás – sticking to any ideology is nuts leads to problems we need to be practical and above all else adapt to current circumstances

Ailbhe – absolutely – adapt to survive

Tomás – is that what you and I have to do in this circumstance in which we find ourselves?

Ailbhe – ah looks like it Tomás love

Ailbhe – let's see what else I can tell you I learnt – well from about 2050 lots of floods – I know there was some when I left the 2020s but we're talking floods man – India, Nepal area especially – Ganges delta – but they move to use hydroelectricity – the Americans are leaders in going out and helping people adapt to environmentalism – 2050s and 2060s the turbulence in Africa really begins to kick off – competition for resources – thanks to the corruption – there and Asia especially, the rapid depopulation due to famine, water shortage, diseases, war –

Irlanda there's a move to growing soft fruits, grapes, olives, figs that kind of thing as southern Europa is too dry to produce enough – trucks will be electric or run on locally-produced fermented type of alcohol from rice or other organic sources – by the 2200s even the early 2100s the drop in population was marked especially in Europa – artificial additives in food was a major problem they found caused cancers and infertility – now there's strict control of population size both in humans and other species – to keep the population manageable but also a consequence of the pollution of the 20th and 21st centuries that has had a 300 year effect on the size of the human breeding cohort – even the pandemics of the 21st and 22nd centuries were a result in part of the alteration of the bacteria caused by the chemical pollution in the 20th and 21st centuries - you must get that the 22nd century suffered terribly because of the pollution and greed of the 20th and 21st centuries – you know the animal species and plants species were already dropping first in our own time, so many species going extinct

Tomás – I get that – when you say it's down from 8 billion people now to half a billion max in your future time = eh?

Ailbhe – oh aye – and there was a rapid drop-off in population in the second half of the 21st century – due to infertility and also then affected by scarcity of resources – female as well as male infertility

Tomás – sounds a very conformist time

Ailbhe – there are a few New Age type communities isolate themselves survivalist types – they tend to want to have weapons and that causes clashes with authorities – then some have settled in artificially enclosed underground cities – I don't see that as very healthy! I've seen them on the news they look sickly no vitamin D or real sunlight

Ailbhe - it took to the early 2200s before scientists really managed to reestablish decent bee and insect populations to support agriculture and the agrarian economy – very little air travel now, eco-friendly airships and ships – I said there aren't big cities now – no need – but also settlements have room for people houses are detached with gardens – people live in communities more it's really so lovely they're so kind and next to no crime – of course a lot of the old cities were lost when the floodwaters rose – rose rapidly, drowning millions but that's another story – like they salvaged the statue of liberty, Chrysler building and empire state building rebuilt them brick by brick miles back inland in the new New York after even the flood defence barriers they constructed failed – like London's – they're trying to reclaim the area where the old London was, get places like the old houses of parliament back up out of the river floodplains like they did with Dublin a while back – in the USA most people live along the coasts the new coastlines we've had since the early to mid 22nd century the interior USA is swathes of prairie or desert, some agriculture but mostly just empty desert – what's left of it – given that the west coast is now at Nebraska, west of that is islands, sandbars or like Florida gone

Ailbhe - we do have clean air again at last now in the last quarter of the 23rd century but the land is still in many places polluted with chemicals and plastics and especially the sea is – we just don't eat fish or anything out of the sea due to the microplastics and toxins – only organic fertilizers are used now – seaweed is cultivated as part of that – of course people are better educated and care about the environment they have to they aren't complacent like people in the 21st century who were focussed on making money and enjoying themselves – now we see the pursuit of happiness as something less self-indulgent and more environment and community based – we know its still going to take decades for the oceans to cleanse themselves of the toxicity that our ancestors like people in your time dumped on us

Tomás – you've every right to blame us babe – what about healthcare

Ailbhe – its much the same – the necessities are provided as part of human rights – some credit charges for some procedures but on the whole its much better – some advances of course like when I first got here you know I got assessed physically and mentally and people get social care and mental health support when its needed

Tomás – what's the big breakthrough in medical science since my time?

Ailbhe – well of the 22nd-23rd centuries I'm not sure exactly when it got perfected but they have a kind of laser diagnosis system to check for physical abnormalities

Tomás – a scanner like Bones McCoy's in *Star Trek*??

Ailbhe – I'm not a trekkie don't know about that but vaguely aware of that and well I know it was as a machine first development on from MRI scanners but yes they've now got handheld ones that are more effective as the decades pass – I do know there is a sonic treatment for blood clots as my friend Jenifa her mam got that done – it breaks down clots – they spotted it early and you see everyone gets an annual in-depth check-up with all the smear tests and so on so things tend to get noticed early and there's less serious issues as a consequence – one thing I miss is profiteroles! there's very little sugar you see – there is a new type of sweetener that is not carcinogenic that's organic but there's just not the same amount of sweet goodies available – people are too sensible! – caner is a lot rarer now the environment has improved – they recognised like trees being carbon sinks that plants can clean the air so they have the right plants in the right places to counter pollution – it's a very plant-based economy – another big advance if you have time to listen, Tomás

Tomás – carry on Ailbhe this is fascinating I'm taking it all in

Ailbhe – I'm a chemist not a physicist but I know time and physics are linked – there's advances in studying the nature of time but unfortunately even my case hasn't led to any publicly acknowledged understanding even if the parapsychologists are more respected now and their work is more widely accepted – in education there are assessments but not quite as exam-based as in our time – I've said before work is seen as service and people tend to study part time after about fourteen-fifteen and also do work or service experience – hence they become more responsible and community minded and independent from an earlier age AND there's less juvenile delinquency and crime in general as there's less social disaffection – but the main thing is children all people in fact are given lots of understanding and love and time so they do alright feel content

Tomás – aren't there still celebrities? entertainers? actors? singers?

Ailbhe – sure but it's a little more muted there isn't the same kind of god-like worship and also none of the celebrity status just for no good reason – though in a way there are programmes to celebrate people in ordinary jobs or situations who have provided extraordinary service and so its truly a global village now

Ailbhe – what else? shopping malls are like they were though more rows of shops in streets covered over to protect from sun or rain and wind but in many shops there are screens and you browse like checking through an Argos catalogue – but still the old-fashioned corner store predominates – a pleasant reversion

Tomás – and you think they understand your situation – they believe that you are from a different time?

Ailbhe – Jon definitely does – he's impressed by the detail I know – when I tell him and friends like Jenifa details, they can tell I'm being honest – I think so anyway

Tomás – hm that's good that's reassuring

Ailbhe – aren't you believed?

Tomás – I'm not sure - and you say people live in a better way too in their relationships with one another – I mean you mentioned how the guy you work with was married

Tomás – Ailbhe?

chapter six – chasing leads

Time passed again and I was not sure if I would ever hear from Ailbhe again. In the meantime, I knew she was gone for good and I should try to get on with my own life. I tried to adjust, move on. Though for a long time I was living as I had after my marriage broke down: surviving really, working, seeing wee Aoife when I could, exercising to be battle fit.

But my obsession continued. My desire to find out what had happened to Ailbhe Gallogly. Was she lost in the mountains that bleak winter, or did she really pass through some portal into another timezone?

I took my mobile back to Aideen at the lab, left it with her.

I spoke to Lieutenant McCarthy, Egan, now my friend despite my being other ranks and his understandable scepticism about my credibility, about this guy Jon Hegarty. My theory was, if Ailbhe was in some daze in our own time and was with some guy Hegarty, if we could trace him we might find her. So Egan researched all the variations of Jon Hegarty he could.

Egan narrowed it down to sixteen suspects. He asked me did I want to help him on Saturdays and Sundays go check them out. He even got Inspector Marty Murphy to go along, since he had civilian authority. We did them in clusters – four a day, over two weekends. Most of them were in Dublin anyway. Most of them were ordinary dudes, with wives or girlfriends, doing boring things at the weekend like playing golf, shopping or watching the kid playing GAA. None had the profile or movements of a potential abductor or conspirator in an elaborate hoax.

Even the one in Killarney, we traced to a mechanic's garage down a rutty old laneway. There he was, under a Ford, tinkering away. The owner came for his vehicle, paid in cash for the new exhaust pipe job.

When the customer was gone, Egan went up to the guy, asked him, 'Are you John Haggarty?'

'Who wants to know?' he replied, wondering why the three of us were interested in him.

'I've a three year old Vauxhall needs a weld.'

'Monday morning.'

'Righto. Suits us grand as the cousins and I've a wake to get to. What'll you be doing the night?'

'Watching Liverpool whip the Arsenal at the Sportsmans.'

We laughed with him as we parted company.

I got promoted to company quartermaster sergeant. Katie Walsh was losing me but I was not going to be far away. She called in a few times to check I was getting on alright.

Eventually, being alone one lunchtime, I asked, 'Is this just a pastoral visit, ma'am, or what?' I leaned close, so that if anything was going to happen, it would happen here and now.

It happened. In that we locked lips.

But she drew back, said, 'I don't take risks at work. Others have.'

'True. And they're history, however much excitement they might've got from it.'

'Is that all this is for you, a bit of excitement?'

'No. Of course not. Though I do like excitement.'

Her eyes twinkled. 'That's good. But I'm due my promotion soon too and I don't want to jeopardise that, so laters honey.'

'And I want you to get your's too, so I won't jeopardise that.'

'Sounds like a promise,' she smootched at me as she left the storerooms office.

I hadn't felt any guilt or remorse after the break-up with the ex, so why did I feel so down now? The lack of closure, I knew instantly. But I just had to keep telling myself Ailbhe herself had pointed out she doesn't get to come back. I'm on my own. More deprived than Lady Chatterley. I should move on. Try to. So I was going to try. Even if Katie didn't turn out to be the real deal, which I suspected she may not, and I may not be for her, I would try to live, not merely survive.

Aideen phoned me at work, said she had completed checking my mobile after the latest texts. 'Can you pick it up tomorrow morning from the lab?' she asked me.

'Is there any chance of me getting it sooner?'

'I'm done here, due to leave now.'

'Do you mind me asking can I meet you somewhere in an hour or so, so I can get it from you, Aideen?'

She hesitated. 'I don't have enormous plans. Can we do this over dinner? What about the Italian south of the park?'

'Sure, Aideen. On me, of course, since I'm putting you out.'

'How long before you're there?'

I was still in Dublin, having met up with Egan, so I told her, 'See you there in half an hour.'

'That'll do.' She was abrupt.

Aideen was already at a table perusing the menu when I arrived ten minutes late. She gave me an annoyed stare. She handed me my mobile as I sat down. I checked it for new messages – there were no more texts – and for charge – 93%, she had kept it up for me.

'Thanks.'

The waiter was straight over. Aideen ordered a pasta dish. I asked for the same without looking at the menu. She asked for a bottle of white without consulting me. I asked for a glass of water, they brought a jug.

'If you think you're going to fuck me because I look like your girlfriend that fell off a mountain dream on, sunshine.'

I shook my head, open-mouthed because I was taken aback by her unexpected, direct comment. Eventually, as she smirked into her first glass of wine, I told her, 'I'm not thinking of anything like that.'

Aideen raised an eyebrow, clearly disbelieving. She poured me a glass of wine. I decided to have it.

'No change in the phone's characteristics? Or the texts?'

'Just the same.'

'If someone, *I,* were faking them, could you tell?'

She snorted. 'Hell yeah. So easy. You'd have to be like ten times better than me to be able to even attempt something like that and even then I could probably suss it was faked even if I couldn't crack them – though I should be able to.'

'Has Egan or Marty Murphy ever asked you do you think I've faked them?'

'Don't need to. They know I'd cover something like that in my reports if it were there.'

'So how do you think these texts are occurring, appearing? Where from?' Aideen thought about it for a moment. 'As I told Egan Walsh, they're genuine and the lack of traceability is unexplainable so the only logical conclusion is that – genuine and unexplainable.'

'You're a rationalist? You're atheist?' I probed.

'I just do what I do.'

'But do you think it *could* be true?'

Aideen stared blankly. She drank another mouthful of wine. 'I'd rather not think about it. If she were to reappear and claim she'd been in another time like,' Aideen lowered her voice, 'the future I might have to actually think about it. Some texts appear on a phone. The person says they are elsewhere. Must be somewhere, unlikely to be a different time just a different place and for some reason the telemetry's warped. Missing.'

'You don't believe it.'

'I don't think you're conning us. She has now claimed so much about this future, whoever the 'she' is that is sending these texts is clearly…'

'Either telling the truth, or lying.'

'Or is deluded.'

'An outside possibly. Let's lump that one in as unwittingly or unconsciously lying, so only the two options. Truth or lie. So you say lie. So Ailbhe must be her or someone else – not me thanks you very much for the vote of confidence – a liar. Lying to me. Winding me up. If a third party, a bit cruel. Who? Only enemy I know of is the ex. Has she conspired with some new guy? But I know from sources she hasn't the support or capacity to do this. Or the imagination, intelligence. Or energy.'

'This is terrible, Tomás, that someone might do this to anyone, to you. That you are in such a tizzy about it, too. I don't expect you to be any other way, but, still, all I can advise you to do is try and forget it. We don't know. Life is full of mysteries. Full of missing people. You're chasing dead-end leads, chasing shadows, chasing rainbows. Just let it go. Even if it is some sick eejit winding you up. Some ex-squaddie you worked with who bears a grudge you are barely perceptible of. If they were going to escalate and do some harm, likely they would have by now.'

'And if it's real?'

Aideen's hand paused before reaching her mouth with a forkful of pasta. 'I don't want to contemplate that. There's no evidence, there's no evidence, there's no evidence.'

my mobile buzzed with a text. We both started! Lifting it, I saw who it was from. 'From my boss!' I laughed. 'From the present. Well, one minute ago already.'

chapter seven – txts from the way back

Tomás – hey Ailbhe if you do ever get back to me could you let me know who wins this and next year's Champions Leagues? or English premiership matches or something like the Champion Stakes or Oaks?

Ailbhe – I'm coming back Tomás
Ailbhe – I've met Jadis a kind of druid shaman lady – she can get me back to my own time – we'll be looking into this – working on it – I hope I will be back with you soon

Ailbhe – hey Tomás – I've told you about the change in attitude towards other species – the reason there was horse races was so people could bet on them but the horses objected so while there are still races there is no betting on it so they are more ad hoc and less of them – so the old races are hard to find anything more than general information on as people just aren't interested anymore – hey Tomás you should see some of the crazy creatures there are now – some of them are a bit like ones we had in the 21st century but evolved a bit – the 21st century saw so many species go extinct, these are either versions of what was left or recreated species through genetic revival like ones that went extinct in the 21st century such as primates and koalas – though of course many species are generally the same or there are old breeds of sheep cattle horses dogs cats etc as well as newer better ones by better I mean adapted to cope with current environmental conditions – like sheep are bigger and woollier as they're bred for their wool now - and they've brought back plant species that were wiped out in your time the 21st century - so anyways no horseracing but I did find out about the football as it still happens just its called the european cup now – the winners of the champions league for 2023-2045 are – *[redacted]* Ailbhe – and here are some unexpected results of premier league matches in 2023-9 seasons – *[redacted]*

Ailbhe - are you there?
Tomás – thanks hon – yes I'm here – when are you coming back?
Ailbhe - ?
Tomás – you txted a white witch is helping you get back
Ailbhe – oh aye – I explored that avenue – Jadis remoteviewed you - I tried but I wasn't able to my psychic strength isn't as good as these 23rd century people
Tomás – she spied on me? what was I doing?
Ailbhe – 4king some blonde
Tomás – not me! I wouldn't do that to you Ailbhe – I didn't cheat on that f Chloe so I'm not going to do it on you – must be from the past
Ailbhe – aw sweet – I would understand if you did we all have needs - I think she did say it was in the future your future
Tomás – won't happen love – she's a fraud
Ailbhe – well as I've said before your devotion is touching – actually there is scientific research into these things – a group got me to go with them to Crauchbán to show them where I believe the portal is and they asked what were the atmospheric conditions what was my state of mind

all that – no joy that time nor since – they accept there are portals and know about them and they understand the quantum physics of them just they haven't managed to artificially create or control one yet – they hope to be able to do so in ten years' time

Tomás – I can wait ten years

Ailbhe – aw Tomás you know I've told you you marry and have a family – I've seen the evidence – it's my dharma to have ended up here and not get back

Tomás – seriously? Ailbhe – I don't want to give up on you

Ailbhe – it's acceptance not giving up

Ailbhe – I go to church now which may sound strange but its not like it was in your time

Tomás – who's pope in 2284? a woman?

Ailbhe – there is a head of christianity and like the world president the top job rotates - annually – among leaders of the various types of faith – but its all one spirituality so no on sees it as remarkable – and there is still a head of a branch of christianity known as pope but it's not a big deal – I think the current one is originally from Venezuela – there have been some female ones sure and married ones and gay or lesbian married ones - but the dominant version of spirituality anyway is a latterday westernised form of hinduism – for a long time it was islam - but the widespread acceptance of the concepts of samsara is part of the global mainstream now – so the pope is just a wee part of it all now and sometimes head of the world temples congress but that rotates regularly – the head of the world temples congress at present is actually the coptic pope, until next month when the head of sikhism gets their turn

Tomás – what other advances are there by the 23rd century?

Ailbhe – in your own century there was the move to decarbonisation though it was slower than it could or should have been hence much of the issues since - despite attempts to force nuclear fusion on the market place as climate change bit hard renewables such as solar and wind power eventually prevailed – there were revolutions in the more authoritarian countries as people wanted a liberal pluralist framework for government – there was an attempt to force ectogenesis on society and impose the perfecting of humanity

Tomás – ectowhat?

Ailbhe – artificial birthing – some believed people were better off designed without imperfections

Tomás – flip nazi or what

Ailbhe – or logic? make smarter fitter people without disabilities or better still have fewer numbnuts why not? but people wanted to have the choice still - and to have the choice to choose what they produce - so there is some ectogenesis but many women still give birth to their own and some men too of course

Tomás – eh??!!

Ailbhe – if I'd a winky eye emoji – just codding you Tomás

Tomás – there have been men who have had babies though through changing gender already

Ailbhe – yeah but apart from that – in this century people are more logical than emotional or hormonal

Tomás – but still family orientated?

Ailbhe – oh sure very very much so but they don't see the discomforts of pregnancy and pain of labour as necessary and more and more are opting for ectopregnancies

Tomás – isn't that maternal closeness lost if the child is from a test tube?

Ailbhe – is it any different for a man if he hasn't borne the child, hasn't he still got a close paternal tie? I discussed this with my friend Jenifa – her grandmother was one of the first to have an ectogenesis birthing – she had two normally first – she said she felt no different having the third one – when they are your's you have the same maternal feeling even if you haven't carried them – I said I would rather carry the child myself I'd feel more of a bond but women now like Jenifa just think why carry it when you can avoid all that hassle and stress on your body – some of her friends were quite snooty really about it, said *why would you want to go through that bestial part?* I asked why bother with sex at all isn't that bestial too which of course their attitude is yes

Tomás – eh?

Ailbhe – they are more Scandinavian, more boring people than in our time – yes they are colder not so touchy-feely – though I like it most of the time – it's reassuring

Tomás – lower sex drive?

Ailbhe – just don't get in the habit of it – more self-controlled – let's see what else would interest you? on one of my climbs recently a friend fell and had an accident lost an eye – they patched her up and I saw her and she was ok and still had sight and I said wtf and she had lost her original eye but no worries they gave her a bionic one – so many diseases have been eradicated btw – no codding this time but there is a guy down our local café has a bionic penis

Tomás – and you know this how?

Ailbhe – everyone knows it – no he doesn't flash it in the café

Tomás – but do you know anyone who's tried it out?

Ailbhe – my friend Jenifa asked him how goes it and he said no complaints – don't know any partners to verify it though

Tomás – does it come with a remote?

Ailbhe – ha-ha

Tomás – are houses automated? do you just get in and say Alexa make me dinner and its ready?

Ailbhe – who would want that?! but there is widespread food preparation as most people don't want to be bothered to cook for themselves – you either order it as you are leaving work and collect it or get it delivered – or eat in a café – not called restaurants anymore just cafés

Tomás – robots and computers didn't take us over then? or overtake us?

Ailbhe – there was a fear they might – they are much more versatile now

Tomás – that'll be the Japanese sex robots 😜

Ailbhe – ha-ha – but no we are in control we don't let the ai take over its not logical that it would it only could if we let it and that would be dumb – it might have happened in the 21st century but not since – some people are more non-biological than biological of course – but wear and tear gets to us all in the end – besides there is acceptance of spiritual recycling or samsara so people aren't so bothered about passing on – er maybe I should point out to you that there is a type of humanoid now developed by us in the early 22nd century that are photosynthetic humans

Tomás – they live off sunlight like plants?

Ailbhe – for a long time the problem was capacity – to generate enough through photosynthesis alone a human would have to be the size of a tennis court and on a dull day you'd feel weak as dishwater – but they developed hybrids first using volunteers then developed it further

Tomás – wee green men literally? or big men

Ailbhe – average sized – don't even need to be green despite adapting the chlorophyl mechanism

Tomás – cool

Ailbhe – interesting aye – though their lifespan is still hit and miss - of course as I've already mentioned there was the rapid depopulation due to famine, water shortages and disease and then the 22nd century wars

Tomás – the hard times and bad times

Ailbhe – one thing you may not be interested in that Jon told me about is people now all have a median artery in their forearm – in your time few have it it's a foetal thing that regresses

Tomás – evolution – but why?

Ailbhe – Jon jokes that compared to the past people nowadays are all wankers lol

Tomás – need a rush of blood to the wrist to avoid passing out?!

Ailbhe – lol

Tomás – or could be because so many do sports like racket sports?

Ailbhe – pass – one thing scientists are still working on but have had some success with is mind uploading – saving all of our mentality to a digital memory – they trace it onto crystal now of course

Tomás – of course

Ailbhe – but while it captures facts and even the character of a person just like say we know what an actor was like from the way they come across in interviews and in their performances it doesn't save the soul – when we physically die we still die and the individual passes on – people now know or believe that uploading of the real individuality is through samsara

Tomás – sounds logical – aren't there still atheists?

Ailbhe – oh yeah sure but church is open to debates and discussions no one is excluded not even doubters and non-believers all views are respected and welcomed philosophical interaction is what it's all about there's no hierarchy of dogmatism

Ailbhe – let's see what else can I tell you – you know the atmosphere didn't recover from the pollution of industrialisation until the end of the 22nd century – the levels of nitrous oxide didn't fall to below what they were at at the beginning of the industrial age that is pre 1750 - four and a half centuries of harm - the two most polluting times in human history were the early industrial revolution period and the late 20th/early 21st centuries period – they were caused by burning fossil fuels and then chemical pollution – birds suffered first, then insects and marine creatures

Tomás – everything sounds very controlled

Ailbhe – at first I thought so – now I realise we're just organised, its simply a matter of responsibility

Tomás – and space exploration?

Ailbhe - oh sure – mostly unmanned probes but there's a long term settlement project of the moon there's hundreds there and they're starting to get to the point where the settlements on Mars are ready for people to go there full-time – Mars is being terraformed – it's a slow process – the moon has been used as the guineapig for that of course and there is quite a lot of development to do - all that is costly and it takes decades centuries to develop the ecology of planets so its long-term stuff but government now is more stable and willing to invest in long-term projects such as improving the environment or this because the individuals aren't such egotists – the scientists are being cautious because some microbes have been found in space and they have to be studied and quarantined to ensure they don't have negative effects here

Tomás – and is there contact with aliens?

Ailbhe – well of course but there was in our time too – only we ordinary plebs weren't told about it officially but the governments – but it was always there – hidden in plain sight

Tomás – I'm waiting for the emoji lol don't know whether that's tongue-in-cheek or not

Tomás – tell me about your daily routine and who you know what new friends you have if any

Ailbhe – sure – I miss Philadelphia my collie – did I tell you I got a dog here? had to plead for a special licence to be allowed one - people have cats to keep the vermin down but very few dogs and virtually no other pets – the practitioner Jon claimed it was for my mental health – so I can take the dog for walks again in the grounds of Muckross House like I used to and Great Connell and by the river where it's so quiet just the cries of ducks and herons rising in the gloaming – bliss – that's my calming places

Tomás – hey, Ailbhe – maybe I'll plant some oaks for you at Muckross

Ailbhe – oh my god Tomás there are big old oak trees there and a couple have hearts carved in them with 2050 and AG TR on them

Tomás – I'll put some in, come back when they're mature in 2050 and do that then lol

Ailbhe – I'm crying like a baby now

Tomás – sorry

Ailbhe – I'll pull myself together - people do run from my new Philadelphia as if she's a wild wolf or something! – but she's sweet as can be – they look at me as if I'm so weird yet the wee kids you meet aren't like that they pet her and hug her and act like children always do around dogs – where is my old Philadelphia?

Tomás – with your mother and father

Ailbhe – I hope you've told them I'm okay

Tomás – I went one afternoon, having tea and scones I told them about the texts – that I'd been with the forensics people and they couldn't be traced – I did say you were ok there – they were polite but I could tell from the looks they were giving me they pitied me thought me off my rocker

Ailbhe – well at least you told them – though it's no comfort to a parent if they haven't their child's body to bury

Tomás – it was a bit like telling them I'd chatted with your ghost – and when I was there at Christmas time, when you first went – they had on the Christmas tree the decoration we got at the Christmas market
Ailbhe – I remember, they were heavy, silver, scrolly, with *Happy Christmas* on them and I put pictures of you and me in them
Tomás – I have the one you gave me on my tree – brings a tear to my eye to see it – they have the other on their's and when I saw it, that was what set me off, blubbering – no wonder they thought I was away with it
Ailbhe – I'm sure they were touched to know you cared so much about their missing daughter
Tomás – I'm sure they think I'm touched! – do they still have Christmas?
Ailbhe – well it's the Yule break now but much like it used to be just more about the winter solstice and new year not specifically christian
Tomás - how do you live love?
Ailbhe – how do you?
Tomás – I get up, jog, eat, go to work, go home, eat, either do more exercise or sit numbly in front of the telly
Ailbhe – surely you go out with your mates
Tomás – occasionally they drag me to the pub when I'm not visiting my wee Aoife
Ailbhe – that's good – you have to go on living, Tomás
Tomás – I try – and you?
Ailbhe – I have said we have the cinema places and sports clubs and church and I eat with friends like Jenifa – my charge is dwindling

Tomás – I will try to get through again – and I will keep trying to find a way to get back home – maybe see if I can find another shaman lady like Jadis who can really help me

Tomás – I understand love – I will try too to find a way through or more about portals or try to create a stargate

Ailbhe – the researchers here have warned me the variables are so great you could pass through to a different time maybe even a different place and time

Tomás – I'd take that risk – to be with you

Ailbhe – so would I hon

Tomás – I miss you I love you

Ailbhe – much love – no matter what

chapter eight – the long and lonesome road

In a way, I was on my way back to normality. I just had not heard from Ailbhe Gallogly much for ages and there was no guarantee she would text again.

Her last conversation, if you could call it that, was about changes since now, that is, our time. It seemed to me she had little to say to me any more, we had little in common any more. She was living a life there, seemed to have got used to it.

She reminded me she knew I moved on eventually, marrying, having a family. Inside, I still believed I would wait seven years, until she was legally declared dead, as if we had been legally married. Or, I would wait ten or more years to see if the people on her side did develop a functioning portal she or I could use. At the same time, I knew this sounded nuts. It might never happen, so why waste years of my life hoping for the virtually impossible? If witchcraft or technology were going to bridge the gap, surely it would have happened by now?

One Friday though, I was having a bitch of a day – little things at work were winding me up, just how my guys were behaving was irritating me. Private Packie O'Neill was being his usual thick self. Filing things in the wrong places. I was storming up the corridor thumping the wall screaming aloud though to myself, 'I'll split that fucker in two with a hatchet!' when Lieutenant Walsh stuck her head round her office door.

'You've all done marvellously this week, great productivity, I'm sending everyone home at two. You slip away now, Tomás.'

Tomás, not sergeant. I knew she was being kind, hoping to calm me down. I did mellow a bit instantly. 'I've a message to do in town right enough, ma'am, thanks, if you don't mind.'

She just nodded, smiled that cat's-got-the-cream-grin of her's and disappeared back to her screen.

By which I meant I had to get a few things in Newbridge before heading home. I had a slow puncture so left the car in at a tyre centre before walking across town to pick up an order from the silverware centre for my dad, for mum's birthday. I popped into TK Maxx for a tee shirt for jogging in, as one of those I was using had ripped when I went to peel it off after a run, it had got so thin. I grabbed a couple of tees and on my way to the paydesk saw a rack of DVDs. I have a player but haven't used it for yonks. If I watch anything I usually watch Netflix not tv. But this one seemed to pulsate, it seemed to be highlighted, drew my attention: *Timecop*. Why? I grabbed it, looked at the back blurb – about a cop – all I took in was *this time-travelling sci-fi thriller* and I took it with me.

After I got back with the car, I jogged. I got a call on my smartwatch from Egan McCarthy.

'Tell me its good news or fuck off.'

'In a bad mood are we? No good or bad news, just touching base, mate.'

'Sorry,' I sighed, catching my breath-rhythm as I jogged.

'Katie told me you were Stormin' Norman this afternoon. All I can offer is a two litre bottle of White Lightning.'

'Sounds good.'

Egan arranged to stop by later.

I took a long, long jog over by the old Great Connell church ruins. Ivy covered stone walls, quite lanes, fields of horses grazing on the stud grounds nearby. Exhaustion calmed me down. For some reason, the evening light flitting through the branches and around the old arches of windows reassured me: I felt as if there is some order, some meaning, even if I couldn't completely comprehend it.

As I jogged near the church ruins, there was a woman ahead of me, with a dog on a lead. From behind some ways, she made me almost have a panic attack: the joggers, the top, the build, the hair: was it Ailbhe?

I sped up, caught up with her. The young woman's dog turned round to watch me unconcernedly as I was overtaking. I stared and stared at the woman's face until I was level, then just past her. She turned her head, turned her face away at that moment, looking at something in the field beyond the hedge. When she looked back, I was clearly staring madly and she was instantly frightened. She gave out a muted cry.

'Sorry, sorry, thought you were someone else,' I tired to reassure her, sped up again till my lungs nearly burst, to get as far away from her as possible so she wouldn't be worried I was some kind of crazy stalker. Of course, it wasn't Ailbhe, just someone with a very vague, distant resemblance to her.

When I got in, I showered, made dinner early – put *Timecop* on in the background as I tended the meal. Watching it, I went from annoyed to perplexed.

I had just switched on the dishwasher when Egan's car pulled up outside. I opened the door before he reached the bell. He was carrying the two litre plastic bottle and a carrier bag. He sat down in the living room as *Timecop* was ending. When it did so, I flicked to a football match and it played in the background with the sound down as we talked.

'Frig'ssake Tomás, you're obsessed.'

'That's true,' I agreed as I handed him two pint glasses. He cracked open the cider and poured. He swung the carrier bag at me, I took out two huge bags of O'Donnell's cheese crisps and a grab bag each of Heroes. 'Haven't you had dinner?'

'Got a sausage supper from the chippy, yeah. But. Still have the munchies.'

'Am I the one in need of a therapy talk or is it you?'

He slugged down half a pint in one go, and so did I.

'I've a thirst because I just ran seven and a half miles.'

'I was at the gym and in the steam room, so I'm parched,' Egan told me.

'You need MiWadi not this.'

'I know what I need.'

'Been dumped?'

'Well, a while ago. But I was living in hope. Now, the hope has gone.'

'Is it like you to care about one particular filly?'

'I thought it was time to settle down.'

'We just don't like being dumped.'

'Or abandoned? It's all a kind of loss. Your loss is different though, I know.'

'Is it? Perhaps, in that there's no certainty. Hey, Egan, in this film *Timecop*…'

'Oh here we go.'

'A guy says you can go back in time but you can't go forward because the future hasn't happened yet.'

'Sounds logical.'

'Yeah, but Ailbhe has gone forward in time. So it's clearly bs.'

'We're suspending judgement, accepting that she has done so, but go on.'

'And though it sounds logical to begin with, but isn't there those who say reality or time-space dimensions is a globe, a network, a mesh, you can weave in and out of, through wormholes?'

Egan wagged a finger. 'Quantum physics. Einstein said the speed of light is absolute so we can't match or pass it as we would meet ourselves coming out on the journey as we're heading back. Some think, I think, that as we approach the speed of light, things start to go funny. Time slows down, or changes. And there's the grandfather paradox – go back in time, prevent your grandfather being conceived, you don't exist, so you can't go back in time to prevent it. Others have thought you enter a parallel universe or state.'

'Agh – my head's gonna explode! So, does this mean a multiplicity of scenarios is possible?'

Egan shrugged, shoulders heavy under the burden of the alcohol as it kicked in.

'Let me postulate – if I exist, even if I go back in time to try to stop my grandfather conceiving – without causing him or my grannie major harm – surely if I go back I must fail, no matter what I try to do, because my existence means my grandfather did conceive and I was also then born.

So, fate or circumstances or whatever you want to call it, will always thwart any attempt I or anyone else tries, as that is the way it is.'

I gesticulated with my arms to question the postulation. All Egan did was offer another of his trademark shrugs, though he did nod too.

Egan said, 'I read up on portals and time travel and that because of Ailbhe's case. A rotating black hole might create the circumstances where it's possible. If somehow some kind of invisible rotating vortex of time occurred in a place, like on Crauchbán, that might explain it. Through some kind of natural or ad hoc or spontaneous process. And some places, like Crauchbán or California's Mount Shasta, are prone to them, to these time portals, so those places are more likely to have the conditions where such a vortex might happen more readily. As in, its not a permanent thing, but the conditions are there for it to occur and disappear and maybe reoccur when the conditions are right. They might be right more often in one place than another. If we could figure out what the conditions are. If they are even the same everywhere, could be a variety of them. And how often do they occur or when in particular places. So we would know when to look for it on Crauchbán. Hm. QED.'

We were swigging away at the cider. Of course, Egan also had some tins of Smithwicks in the carrier bag. He was really going for it. We were both burbling.

Egan told me, 'I saw a documentary recently where a corporal in Chile approached a light that he and his platoon thought was a UFO. He seemed to be swallowed up by it. A few minutes later, as it seemed to his platoon, he came back. But he had beard growth and his watch read five days into the future. He didn't recall anything.'

'Like in *Men In Black*, the aliens wipe your memory!' We giggled and tittered like schoolboys.

'Stories like *The Time Machine* and *A Christmas Carol* have characters like Scrooge who see the past and future.'

'Ack!' I scoffed, 'I'm not interested in fiction. I want to know can it be real?'

'Again, we're postulating, if we go into the future, we can't change the past of what happens, because destiny or whatever you want to call it won't let us. It's predetermined, if not completely then as far as any interference from time travellers is concerned. QED. Theoretically, so the current researchers say, we can go to the past, yes, through a means of exceeding the speed of light such as through wormholes, cosmic strings or Alcubierre drives.'

'Whatever they are. Beer drives?' I joked.

'Alcubierre. Basically warp drive, as in *Star Trek*. Create an energy-density field lower than that of vacuum, so you get negative mass, hey presto. Cosmic strings are one-dimensional topological defects when vacuum manifolds are associated with symmetry breaking.'

'It was one dimensional defects like Packie O'Neill made me lose my rag today, want to break his symmetry. Again, theoretical. Fictional!'

'Plausible. Basically you just bend the space-time continuum and slip through. Haven't you heard about Project Pegasus?'

When I shook my head, Egan went on, 'An American dude has been claiming for years his dad was part of a secret American government project and he, as a kid in 1972, got sent back to watch Lincoln give the Gettysburg Address in 1863, and he's in a photo taken at the time.'

I whistled.

'They used technology developed by Nikola Tesla, where a curtain of radiant energy is created, which can bend space-time. The dude who was involved by his dad as a kid even went back twice to the same place and time and there were two of him there at the same time.'

I was shaking my head. 'Such brave guys, using their kids as guineapigs.'

'Naw, they worked out it was easier for youngsters to do the travelling.'

'Hm, yeah right. In *Timecop*, when you go back, if you meet your past self, they say you can't touch yourself because the same matter can't inhabit the same space-time. So, when the bad dude is thrown against his past self in *Timecop,* he melds into this lump of jellylike mush.'

'My aunt claims to have the second sight, but she's quite a trendy chick, new agey, and neo-pagan. Anyway, our Crystal does oracle card reading and says she's clairaudient and can tell people about past and future lives. And she said to me once when I came out of a trance she'd put me in I'd said of this life I'm ninety-eight percent here, and I said where's the other two percent and she said, resting. And at times we can be in more than one place-time. So spiritualists tend to agree with the physicists.'

'And Ailbhe would agree – would say they're more spiritual in the future as well as more scientific.'

'Reality isn't necessarily linear, is it?'

'But what about these paradoxes and quandries? Like in *Timecop*, if some bad dude goes back in time and steals technology, so say the Allies don't get the atom bomb in nineteen-forty-five, but someone else keeps it till their time in the future, does Hitler win? Or if the Allies still win, does someone else in the future, like Saddam Hussein or Putin?'

'Or, if you kill Hitler in nineteen thirty-one, does that make the future worse instead of better? Or do we know it didn't happen because here we are and we know it didn't happen? So that can't be changed?'

'Or if it was, would this just be one of many possible or actual existences, a parallel time universe?'

'You answered it yourself, saying however much we might try to interfere, we might not always be able to. Circumstances might thwart our efforts to change things.'

'Whatever alternatives there are, I think the universe, or my world anyway, would be better with Ailbhe in it.'

'But would it?' Egan snapped morosely, cracking open a tin and drinking straight from the can. 'Am I better off without yer wan who decided I wasn't right for her? Wasn't she right and I wrong? Would Ailbhe have stayed with you much longer or you with her if she hadn't disappeared when she did? All we can know is, she's gone. Whatever the reason is. You're on your todd. And so am I. And we just have to pick up the pieces and get on with life.'

'I try. I try,' I tried to tell him. 'Aren't I raging as you are because I'm thwarted. But maybe I should be more resigned because I should accept fate, destiny, not try to change it because it's not maybe meant to be changed? In *Timecop* they reckon time travel is the biggest threat to the world since the nuclear bomb. I can well believe it. In that film, they try to police it, control it, even shut it down. If it is possible, if Americans or someone else did manage to do it in the past, or currently can, no wonder they would suppress it, try to hide that it can be done.' My head was spinning now, with the alcohol. 'What's the truth, Egan?' I moaned.

'You want the truth? Can you handle the truth?' He gawfawed, having mimicked Jack Nicholson.
We laughed.
'Ailbhe dropped into things that I carve on trees in 2050. Now I'm wondering why? Of course I will try to make it a self-fulfilling prophecy, but why that year? Does she know something I don't? She's been to my grave. What year does it say on it? Do I make it to 2052? Is that a personal thing or is this rapid drop off of population she predicts in the second half of this century something to do with it? Widespread sickness, or starvation through resource scarcity?'
Egan just shook his head in a minimalistic fashion and we drank the last of the beer and tucked into our snacks, before crashing, me in my cold room, Egan in the spare.

Egan was still there snoring his head off the next morning when my mobile rang. I grabbed for it on the bedside table, wondering could it be Ailbhe getting through?
'Hello?'
'Tomás. Katie Walsh here. I hope you don't mind me ringing you on your day off, on a Saturday.'
'Not at all.'
'Just yesterday you seemed to be, well, upset.'
'Oh, just a mood. Had a few beers and I've more to feel sorry about this morning.'
'Oh dear.'
'Well, not that many, ma'am. Still good to go a run, clear the head.'

'Oh, well, actually I tend to jog myself Saturdays. There's actually a park run in an hour, if you want to join me on that?'

'Eh. Yeah, sure. Good idea. I would usually do my own route and have peace but a park and crowd of ones, no worries, it's all good.'

She told me where and when to meet to start. I downed a coffee, had a shower to rid myself of the beeriness. Egan was emerging from the curtain-dulled room as I grabbed my car keys.

'You're a bit late for the park run but if you want to throw on some trainers there's still time to just make it.'

He held up a hand. 'I had a lot more than you, mate. I won't be running today.'

I left him to his hangover and drove to the leisure centre car park where the race was to begin. There weren't too many there so I found Katie easily enough just as they were about to set off.

Katie knew some of the ones there so introduced us as we jogged, and we all chatted smalltalk as we wend our way along the paths among the trees.

It was invigorating to be among likeminded people and to see the kid who fell off his bicycle at the end of his first unaided ride get congratulated at the same time as being comforted because he scraped a knee.

After the five miler, I asked Katie, 'Coffee?'

'Well, I could shower here…'

'You're fine!'

So she went to the café in the leisure centre with me. I got a large water as well as coffee, same for her, and I asked for chips to soak up what was left of the alcohol whereas Katie just asked for a scone.

So we talked and talked, laughed and joked. I realised halfway through our sit there that something was happening. I felt guilty and yet in the back of my mind I knew Ailbhe had been encouraging me to move on. I realised I had got to the point where nothing really mattered anymore, I just wanted to be alive and live.

When we were walking back out to the car park, I said to Katie, 'I usually jog down by the old ruined church.'

'I'm not familiar with it.'

'Could show you it now, if you like?'

Katie smiled, gave a half-nod, joined me in my car. It was only a few minutes drive to the gateway with the white board sign arched above it, in English and Irish, black crucifix, the overgrown path leading to half-hidden gravestones and the small, rectangular, roofless derelict building beyond.

The year above the sign read 1736. More than two hundred and sixty years ago. So about the span that now separated Ailbhe and me, I thought. If I had looked it up at the time I would have found out that at that time Benjamin Franklin was starting the first fire brigade in Philadelphia, Robert Walpole was moving into Downing Street in London, the Ottoman Empire was ascendant and Berkeley was wondering how foreigners could believe half the population of Ireland were dying of hunger when the country was so abundant in foodstuffs. It was, of course, because, having stripped the island of timber, the landlords were raking it in exporting meat and dairy products to fuel the British navy and support the slave plantations in the West Indies.

As we walked through the long grass there, we did not know how many unmarked graves there might be from a few years after the opening of the place, when a famine ended the lives of nearly half a million. There would be another, even greater famine a century after that, and a century after that it would be the Emergency and great depression when more went hungry. It would be another century before slavery was abolished by that empire, longer in other parts of the world.

But I did wonder how much we had progressed in that time span? I was living in a world where economic hardship was hitting hard. If not as widespread or as bad, nonetheless many were again facing cold and hungry times. And the worst thing about it all, that panic that grips when you realise you can't pay a bill and the desperation, the same wild fear that tossed so many from high windows a century ago.

I did think of what Ailbhe had said about her future world, how at last freedom from need and a fairness in the distribution of life's necessities was universally applied. No wonder she was content therethen. Did we really progress by babysteps, so slowly righting one wrong, then the next? Would we ever as a species sort ourselves out, organise ourselves on this planet so that we really treated all of us with dignity and respect? It was selfish of me to want to drag Ailbhe away, back from that better life. They say sometimes if you really love someone you have to let then go, go their own way.

We had walked to the church. A railed grave and other headstones were shaded by a big old tree that was clearly as old as this cemetery and church.

'It's peaceful here, relaxing in a creepy sort of way,' Katie turned to say to me. She smiled.

Our eyes met and we both moved at the same time, towards each other, to kiss. And then we were embracing, caressing, as we kissed. It was as if it was always meant to be. It lasted an eternity.

But when at last we did break for breath, laid our faces against each others' shoulders, Katie whispered, 'We could go to your's,' I jolted back, held her at arm's length, shook my head nervously.

'Eh, that's not really a good idea.'

She frowned. 'Have you got someone there?'

'Well, hmm, Egan.'

'Egan McCarthy? Well you're a dark horse.' Katie stepped back from me completely then.

'Not like that. He called round for a chat. Trying to cheer me up. And with the latest non-news from forensics. And brought cider. And.' I shrugged the way Egan would.

Katie shook as she laughed, her amusement infectious.

'We'll get a room!' I enthused. 'The Keadean or someplace.'

'We can go to mine. I was just being cautious. And the place is a tip.'

'Nonsense.'

'Why did you bring me *here*?' she suddenly asked.

'I found it by accident, jogging out this way. the arable fields, the stud, this picturesque ruin.'

Katie pointed to a gravestone. It read *Walsh*. I gasped. 'I didn't know.' She nodded, smiled, walked back towards the gateway, me following.

That was how it began. I did say to her, that weekend, about her being an officer, me a non-commissioned. She pointed out other couples in the same position, over the years. She did say before long we would have to declare ourselves to line management, we could not be in a relationship and working together for long. At least I was already in a different office, I reminded her, having got the recent promotion. We even discussed the longer term: would I try for a commission? Would one or both of us look outside the service for private sector employment?

I thought that first flush of romance might dwindle, might soon extinguish. And through it all I tried not to think of Ailbhe. It wasn't my fault she had gone. If she were to come back now? That was my main thought: perhaps I was tempting fate and that was what would happen – Katie would get pregnant, or we'd marry, and then up Ailbhe would pop again.

I had to decide, definitively, now. I had to commit so there was no going back. Choose between the living and the – what, the not-yet born? Or at least she who was claiming to be living in a time not yet born.

And then it happened.

One Thursday evening Katie was driving us home from work, from the camp. Katie had let out her place, we were in mine.

'Let's eat out.' She suggested we go to the Keadean's restaurant.

'What's the occasion?'

'Just, treat ourselves.' She had an enigmatic smile.

'This isn't the way,' I pointed out, realising in the dark evening we were heading in the opposite direction.

'Going the scenic way, it's a loop. Ten minute detour.'

She pulled up at Great Connell churchyard and got out. I followed her through the gate into the moonlit, overgrown grounds. She stopped along the path, near the big old tree.

'What's going on?'

'Will you marry me?'

I rocked on my boot heels. She waited silently for an answer as I hesitated. 'Yes!' I blurted out.

'I asked you because I knew you'd have difficulty asking me. But it's a leap year, so I can.' She took out a ring box and put it in my hand. I passed it back to her, opening it with a flourish to expose the diamond ring glinting in the moonlight. Katie took it and put it on her finger, showed it off to me.

'If you're sure this is what you want.' She nodded. I told her, 'I know it's taken me time to get over, losing Ailbhe. But I swear, Katie, I am committing to you and I will focus completely on you.'

'I understand you can't just switch off feelings. Especially when there was never a body to bury.'

'And with Chloe, you know it was her doing, that…'

Katie silenced me with a hand on my mouth. 'I wouldn't be asking you if I didn't have confidence in you.'

'And you have a degree and are commissioned, whereas I…'

'Are the most intelligent, wisest, kindest, decent man I've come across.'

'Wow,' I lowered my head, genuinely shocked, not expecting praise.

'I am ready,' I told her. 'To move on.'

'Round Christmas time, I went with my aunt and step-uncle to the cemetery, to lay flowers at her first husband's grave. He died in the pandemic. I asked her new husband what it was like for him, seeing her devotion to this dead man. He told me, we should love others, like family, even friends, we should love as many as possible. I said isn't this kind of love different? He said, she spent her life with him, they made a promise, until death us do part, so she is free to love him, but he doesn't expect her not to still love someone else. We've all loved in the past, unless we're hermits. We've all been rejected, or dumped, or hurt, or have lost. But we make a commitment here and now, to someone, here and now.'

I finished it for her, 'And we don't let the past or the future impinge on that.'

Katie nodded. We walked back to the car, went for dinner. Which now I realised was a celebration dinner.

And I felt at ease with it all.

chapter nine – I'll write your name through the fire

Tomás – hey Ailbhe are you there?

Tomás – hey, I did it – I planted oak saplings in the grounds of Muckross House. Yup someday I'll go back, carve our initials on them – you keep saying I'll marry – doesn't she go before me? do I carve our initials on the trees after she's gone?

Tomás – when I walk there, I think of you

Tomás – I'm in Killarney as much as I can be now

Tomás – hey Ailbhe thanks to you I'd a big win on the champions league match – 14/1 outsiders and I put on a hefty whack – I'm gonna put it by as a stake for the next big one – as well as a number of premier league wins – all thanks to you Ailbhe – if you need me to do something for you – leave something hidden say that's new now but worth loads in your time?

Tomás – hey Ailbhe I was thinking it there are aliens there could you not ask them to leave you back here in this time? A mate was saying they take people into their spacecraft and five days pass but they leave the person back minutes after they were taken maybe with amnesia but wouldn't it be worth it to get back? you've been away awhile but you could turn up a year after you went and with amnesia no one would ask where have you been they'd just go ok you're back and pick up where you left off?

Ailbhe – hi Tomás – yeah I'd love to pick up where I left off but I asked Jon who asked a guy he knows in the government and they said if there are aliens, which he would neither confirm nor deny, then the aliens have this policy of not interfering – least not any more than they have to - and they didn't cause me to be herenow so they won't get involved and try and help me get back – of course I asked what about any government projects into this kind of thing haven't they been doing it or trying to do it for years and he said the same thing hear no evil see no evil speak no evil do no evil – huh – looks like the only way is back through the fire the light flash of the portal on Crauchbán – and I keep trying – keep climbing and going by the place and all round the summit – not just to enjoy the view of Kerry from up there but also to try and reach you

Ailbhe – and Tomás no I don't need anything in this time – we have all that we need – as I've said before plenty to go round – only half a billion people at most on the planet nowadays – like it says on the Georgia Guidestones – regions and the world do tend to be governed by these general principles nowadays – we have an age of reason – though I get lonely at times – but I have Philadelphia best pooch – Tomás – Tomás

Ailbhe – thanks for planting the oak trees! – don't forget in 2050 you carve our initials on them xx – oh yeah you say you will

Ailbhe - damn Tomás I was up Crauchbán again today along the pass where I got zapped – hoping to pass back through the fiery flash of light and get back there – no joy today sigh

Ailbhe – I suspect you will agree between us there's no need for intense chats because we sense the strength of this connection – all we need to do is know we're there for each other – unfortunately we can't enjoy each other's company – fate has intervened to prevent that and our time for that has been cut short – but as Hardy once wrote, *experience is as to intensity not as to duration* – it was good while it lasted hon – such a formidable chemistry between us – you are and will always be the best friend I could ever wish for – it's a higher love for sure – your being there for me has made this transition so much easier for me – have I come to terms with being herenow? I guess so – have I given up on ever getting back 'home' – hmmm not quite – all the same, do I love it here, hell yes

Tomás – hell did I miss you Ailbhe!? are you there now? I was in a bloody work meeting

Ailbhe – hey Tomás
Tomás – Ailbhe! Ailbhe! I'm here
Ailbhe – gotcha Tomás – how's you?
Tomás – I'm well – I checked up on your family for you too
Ailbhe – aw thanks sweetie – how's mam – I'd a dream about her

Tomás – I'm afraid I've some bad news there – Ailbhe your mum had a heart attack and passed on – it was sudden – but quick and painless
Ailbhe – sigh – is it that time there already? – it's rough hearing that – thanks for letting me know – how's daddy coping?
Tomás – soldiering on – he's okay – misses her like crazy of course
Ailbhe – as I do – but in a way I already knew – I've been to their grave after all – I've seen the dates, knew it wasn't long after I transitioned here that that happened – good send off?
Tomás – oh yes beautiful service - your sister's engaged though – some good news – omg Ailbhe this is such big dreadful news and all I can do is offer a few words of sympathy
Ailbhe – it's okay – as I say I know she would go about now – that's splendid news about the engagement! pass on my sorrow and my joy – and you Tomás what have you been up to?
Tomás – yeah though I know its awkward for your family – I think maybe I should leave them to their own coming to terms not bother them again - and apart from that I'm not up to much just working away – I spoke to my line manager about redeployment – got itchy feet see
Ailbhe – to a danger zone?
Tomás – more front line, yeah, for maybe one last time – don't fret pet – I'm just bored with the kind of admin role they have me doing – so she's looking into it – I said when I'm busy my mind's off things – even taking a class through basic training that's my second choice
Ailbhe – that would be cool
Tomás – long days and hard graft but you get to see them progress blossom become real soldiers

Ailbhe – like rearing a child in a few months instead of years

Tomás – well the last bit anyways – more moulding professionals - I just want to do something active again before I start leaving it too late and can't any more

Ailbhe – you're young yet! and fit

Tomás – thanks babe but you know what I mean – I have even been toying with the idea of leaving altogether, starting up some wee business – but you what have you been doing or learning recently

Ailbhe – sounds like you're thinking of settling down

Tomás – oh no not yet awhile

Ailbhe - well like most people I have my vegetable garden and it's not as accomplished as other's here but I'm learning

Tomás – cool – I must start one sometime soon – my grandad grew his own spuds and they were amazing organic tasty

Ailbhe – and the rest – peas, beans, onions, carrots, sprouts, radish, beetroot, lettuce

Tomás – omg Ailbhe – and any excitement?

Ailbhe – a guy at work told me of an old house that was being cleared and they had a load of boxes of musty old books and they said I could have them they'd just get incinerated as people now read online but the feel of a real book in your hand, turning the page, you can't beat it - and they were in a pretty bad state spines gone really yellowed and brittle but I took them anyway so I've been reading my way through some old favourites and some new to me – Austen, Hardy, Brontës, Kafka, Camus, Pavese, Calvino, Huxley, McGahern, Morrison,

Atwood, Woolf, Ferrante, Le Guin, Lee, Orwell, Capote, Leitch, Pamuk, Macken, Vonnegut, Sagan, Zola, aw!

Tomás – some hoard

Ailbhe – delicious

Tomás – you weren't always a reader

Ailbhe – well when younger – at school – after that working and socialising and climbing and watching movies got in the way

Tomás – it's all we boil down to eh? – like physically we are just so many grams of this chemical and that powder, the self is just so many memories and so much passing time – the physical self gets stimulated by food and comfort and sex and exercise and relaxation and sleep and the inner self gets stimulated by emotional cues from movies and books and music

Ailbhe – ah but the whole is way greater than the sum of the parts

Tomás – true - do you ever get away for a holiday

Ailbhe – as I've said there's not much distant travel people just don't bother don't want to affect the environment and know there's as much good stuff near home as far away – and people herenow tend to go to walk or see places of interest – I got a trip across to what was Yorkshire – saw Brontë country – the parsonage – still a museum – I enjoyed that even if I know I don't need to go there really can understand and appreciate it just as much from reading about it and looking at pictures and virtual walkthroughs – I love the buffeting of the wind against your face as you look across the desolate moors

Tomás – if you went then I will go some time soon too

Ailbhe – you don't have to just because I did

Tomás – it makes me feel closer to you – to be somewhere I know you've been
Ailbhe – aw that's nice – but it's also okay if we drift apart
Tomás – don't say that
Ailbhe – isn't it inevitable? star-crossed lovers and all that?
Ailbhe - I thought you'd be married by now – if you want a hint to help you Tomás your gravestone says your wife's name was
Tomás - don't
Ailbhe – K
Tomás – don't tell me!
Ailbhe - K - I won't
Tomás – I get by here – a lot of the time I'm not sure what I need – I know I cocoon myself from the world from people
Ailbhe – you say you get by – you mean you survive but I wonder is it really living? Life is like a bubble, it's been turned inside out on me and it's as if I am on the outside looking in – and I realise the important ingredient that's required is simply love – you mentioned child rearing but I see the main thing they - others – people herenow especially young ones - seem to have more of is time – more time from parents or carers, teachers, other mentors in the community – and that makes such a difference – I go now to help with a schools after hours development programme – it's like Gaisce
Tomás – I feel similar – I will go soon and do something similar, help out with the scouts or something – try and lift myself when I feel down by focussing on others not wallow in self-pity

Ailbhe – I know you probably think it's lame here, boring, but there's so much love, it's overwhelming – the only love that's missing is that we can't be together anymore

Ailbhe – don't be down Tomás – try to attract positivity by being positive – even if you have to as it were pretend at first – try and it'll come – because you know life is short and is precious and we should make the most of the time we have not mope around wondering what if or if only or when when when

Tomás – I keep trying to tell myself that Ailbhe

Ailbhe – and you know it's not so bad here, in fact I prefer it in so many ways – as I've said before the main thing is just that people like daddy and the rest of them and you aren't here

Ailbhe – and you gave me bad news and I have some for you Tomás – in that I was up Crauchbán with the climbing club a while ago and I had a wee fall –

Tomás – Ailbhe!

Ailbhe – I'm in one piece sort of – but I'm in a chair now – they can fix a lot of things herenow but not this – trust me to bust something that can't be repaired – anyways I can work, get about, may still be able to have children even but climbing up snowy pinnacles is one thing that's out for good – I'll have to admire them from a distance from now on

Tomás – omg Ailbhe!

Ailbhe – I'm ok with that – so don't be worrying about me Tomás – you get on with living your own life – even if I can't get back to the portal place to try and return

Tomás – I can still go there – can still try to get where you went

Ailbhe – it's such a longshot Tomás – don't bust a gut or like me bust your back trying

Tomás – well I still will keep trying Ailbhe - no matter what

Ailbhe – and I will in my own way – keep hoping too – no matter what

Ailbhe – no matter what else I do or you do I know what we have had is real and wonderful and infinite and eternal and I will always be here for you think know you will you be there for me

Tomás – yes Ailbhe yes I will yes

postscript – no matter what

After that, the texts from Ailbhe ceased to arrive. Neither I nor anyone else has heard from her since.

A while ago, too, my mobile phone died on me. I took it to the shop and they got it going again. When they did, though, when I got it back all my messages and recorded voice messages were gone. The shop's techies tried to retrieve things but could not, inexplicably even my backup was all lost as irrevocably as the DMs of a government minister facing an enquiry. So all my texts to and from Ailbhe were gone. I don't even have them anymore, to cherish, except in transcript form. I took my mobile to my friend Aideen in the forensics lab, to see if she could retrieve them. No joy.

I won big betting on the Champions League and other matches, bought a house on the outskirts of Killarney, have my notice in to leave the army. Yes, I married Katie, yes we have a baby now – Katie suggested we call her Ailbhe, I declined, suggested Molly after both our grandmothers instead. Even though I focus now on them, I must confess at times in my leisure time I climb Crauchbán occasionally, hoping to either pass through the portal to 2284 or meet Ailbhe coming back.

So far, I haven't had any luck but we'll see what today's excursion brings. And if I do not find her today, even if I never get any more texts from Ailbhe ever again, even though deep down inside I know she was trying to tell me she knew all too well it will never happen, regardless, I will wait for her until the end of time, I will love her until all things end and beyond. No matter what.

Tomás Roe
Killarney, Ireland
30th December 2024

MacGillycuddy's Reeks, County Kerry, Ireland

About the author

Niall McGrath is a Pushcart Prize nominated writer from County Antrim, N Ireland. His poetry selections include *Shed* (2021, Lapwing, N Ireland), *Clay* (2013, Lapwing, N Ireland), *Treasures of the Unconscious* (2009, Scotus Press, RoI), *Reversion* (2003, Sixties Press, UK) and *Godsong & A Matter of Honour* (2000, Black Mountain Press, N Ireland). His novels include *The Way of Tenderness* (2015, A&M, London) and *Sanctuary* (2024, Black Spring Press, London).